Edmund Hodgson Yates

Black Sheep

A novel. Vol. 1

Edmund Hodgson Yates

Black Sheep
A novel. Vol. 1

ISBN/EAN: 9783337245405

Printed in Europe, USA, Canada, Australia, Japan

Cover: Foto ©Andreas Hilbeck / pixelio.de

More available books at **www.hansebooks.com**

BLACK SHEEP.

A Novel.

BY

EDMUND YATES,

AUTHOR OF "KISSING THE ROD," "THE FORLORN HOPE," ETC.

"Love is strong as death; jealousy is cruel as the grave."

IN THREE VOLUMES.

VOL. I.

LONDON:

TINSLEY BROTHERS, 18 CATHERINE ST. STRAND.

1867.

In Memory

OF

"THE GROWLERY."

CONTENTS OF VOLUME I.

BLACK SHEEP.

" I'm to keep to the right ?"

" Keep on a bearin' to the right, sir, 'cross Watch Common, and down One Ash Hill, and that'll bring you straight on to Poynings, sir! No luggage, sir?"

" None, thank you!"

" Luggage! no! I should think not! party's without a overcoat, don't you see, Thomas?— without a overcoat, and it freezin' like mad! Poynings, indeed! What's he doin' there? He don't look much like one of the company! More like after the spoons, I should say!"

The polite porter who had made the inquiry,

and the satirical station-master who had commented on the reply, remained gazing for a minute
or two at the stranger who had just arrived at
the Amherst station of the South-Eastern Railway, and then went back to the occupations from
which the premonitory whistle had called them;
which, in the porter's case, consisted of a retire-
ment to a little wooden watch-box where, surrounded by oil-cans, grease-boxes, dirty swabs of
cloth, and luggage-barrows reared on end and
threatening with their fore-feet, he proceeded to
the mending of his shoes with a bit of tin and
a few tacks, while the station-master turned to
the accounts which extracted the marrow from
his very soul, and carried on what he called the
"tottle" of a drove of two hundred and sixty
oxen, conveyed at per head.

"Freezing like mad." The station-master was
right. The frost, which of late years holds aloof,
utterly destroying the pictorial prophecies of the
artists of the illustrated periodicals regarding
Christmas Day, and which, with the exception
of a two days' light rime, had left January a
moist and muggy month, had set in with the

commencement of February, hard, black, and evidently lasting. The iron-bound roads rang again, even under the thin boots of the stranger, who hurried over them with a light and fleeting step. The sharp keen air whirling over bleak Watch Common so penetrated his light, London-ish clothing, that he shivered horribly, and, stopping for an instant, beat his sides with his hands in an awkward manner, as one to whom the process was new, and who was vainly en-deavouring to imitate some action he had seen. Then he hurried on with a short rapid jerking step, essentially different from the league-swallow-ing swinging pace of the regular pedestrian ac-customed to exercise; stumbling over the frozen solid ruts made by the heavy cart-wheels, slipping on the icy puddles, and ever and anon pausing to take fresh breath, or to place his hand against his loudly beating heart. As he skirted the further edge of the common, and arrived at the brow of the hill which the porter had mentioned to him, and which he recognised by the solitary tree whose branches rustled above him in the night wind, he heard, by the chimes of a distant church,

ten o'clock rung out sharp and clear through the
frosty air. He stopped, counted each chime, and
then set off again at a quickened pace, his progress down the descent being easier now, muttering to himself as he went:

"Ten o'clock! I must press on, or they'll all
be in bed, I suppose. Beastly respectable, old
Carruthers, from what I can make out from my
mother, and what little I saw of him! Servants
up to prayers and all that kind of thing. No
chance of getting hold of her, if I can't make her
know I am there, before those prayers come off.
Glass of cold water and flat candlestick directly
they're over, I suppose, and a kiss to Missy and
God bless you all round, and off to bed! By
George, what a life! What an infernal, moping,
ghostly, dreary existence! And yet they've got
money, these scoundrels, and old Carruthers could
give you a cheque that would make you wink.
Could! Yes, but wouldn't, especially to me! Ba,
ba, black sheep, and all the rest of it! Here's a
poor tainted mutton for you, without the wind
being in the least tempered to him! Jove, it goes
through me like a knife! There'll be a public

somewhere near, I suppose, and when I have seen my mother, I'll step off there and have some hot rum-and-water before turning in. Hold up, there, you hawbuck brute, pull your other rein! What's the use of your lamps, if they don't show you people in the road?"

He had sprung aside as he spoke, and now stood flat against and pushing into the leafless hedge as a carriage with flashing lamps and steaming horses whirled so closely by him as almost to brush his arm. The coachman paid no attention to his outcry, nor did the footman, who, almost hidden in overcoats, was fast asleep in the rumble behind. The next instant the carriage was whirling away; but the pedestrian, seeing the condition of the footman, had swung himself on to the hind step, and, crouching down behind the rumble and its unconscious occupant, obtained a shelter from the bitter wind, and simultaneously a lift on his road. There he crouched, clinging firmly with both hands in close proximity to the enshrouded knees of the unconscious footman— knees which, during their owner's sleep, were very helpless and rather comic, which smote each other in the passage of every rut, and occasionally parted and displayed a dreary gulf of horsecloth between them, to be brought together at the next jolt with a very smart concussion—and there he remained until the stopping of the carriage, and a sharp cry of "Gate" from the coachman, induced him to descend from his perch, and to survey the state of affairs from that side of the carriage most removed from a certain light and bustle into which they had entered. For, on the other side of the carriage to that on which the stranger stood, was an old-fashioned stone lodge with twinkling lights in its little mullioned windows, and all its thousand ivy-leaves gleaming in the carriage-lamps, and happy faces grouped around its door. There was the buxom lodge-keeper the centre of the group, with her comely red face all aglow with smiles; and there was her light-haired sheep-faced husband standing by the swinging iron gates; and there were the sturdy children, indulged with the unwonted dissipation of "sitting up;" and there was the gardener's wife awaiting to see company come in, while her master had gone up to look at fires in hothouses; and there were

Kidd, the head keeper, and little Tom, his poor idiot boy, who clapped his hands at the whirling lights of the carriages, and kept up an incessant boom of imbecile happiness. Sheep-faced male lodge-keeper bobbing so furiously as to insist on recognition, down goes window of carriage furthest from the stranger, and crisp on the night air cries a sharp curt voice,

"How do, Bulger? Not late, eh? hum—ah! not late?"

To which Bulger, pulling at invisible lock of hair on forehead:

"No, Sir Thomas! Lots company, Sir Thomas! Seasonable weather, Sir—"

But the carriage was whirled away before Bulger could conclude, and before the stranger could resume his place under the sheltering lee of the now conscious footman. He shrank back into the darkness—darkness deeper and thicker than ever under the shadow of the tall elms forming the avenue leading to the house, and remained for a minute buried in thought.

The night was clear, and even light, with the hard chilly light of stars, and the air was full of

cold—sharp, pitiless, and piercing. The wind
made itself heard but rarely, but spared the way-
farer not one pang of its presence. He shrank
and shivered, as he peered from under the gaunt
branches of the trees after the carriage with its
glittering lights.

"Just like my luck!" he thought, bitterly.
"Nothing is to be wanting to make me feel myself
the outcast that I am. A stranger in my mother's
house, disowned and proscribed by my mother's
husband, slinking like a thief behind the carriages
of my mother's fine friends. I will see my mother,
I must see her; it is a desperate chance, but
surely it must succeed. I have no doubt of *her*,
God bless her! but I have my doubts of her power
to do what I want."

He emerged from the shadow of the trees
again, and struck into the avenue. He quickened
his pace, shivering, and seeing the long line of
way lying level before him in the sombre glimmer
of the night, he went on with a more assured
step. Angry and bitter thoughts were keeping
the young man company, a gloomy wrath was in
his dark, deep-set eyes, and the hands which he

thrust into his coat-pockets clenched themselves with an almost fierce impatience. He strode on, muttering, and trying to keep up an air of hardihood (though there was no one to be deceived but himself), which was belied by the misgivings and remorse at his heart.

"A fine place and a grand house, plenty of money, and all that money gives, and no place for her only son! I wonder how she likes it all! No, no, I don't; I know she is not happy, and it's my fault, and HIS." His face grew darker and more angry, and he shook his clenched hand towards a stately house, whose long lighted façade now became visible.

"And *his—his* who married my mother and deceived her, who gave her hopes he never intended to fulfil—my ill conduct the cause of his forbidding her to bring me here!—he always hated me; he hated me before he saw me, before he ever knew that I was not a sucking dove for gentleness, and a pattern of filial obedience and propriety; he hated me because I existed—because I was my mother's son; and if I had been the most amenable of step-sons, he would have hated me all the same, only he would have shown his hatred differently, that's all. I should have been brought here, and made to feel insignificance, instead of being left to beg or starve, for all he cares. I am better off as it is."

A harsh smile came over his face for a moment. "Quite a blackguard, and all but a beggar. All but? No, quite a beggar, for I am coming to beg of my mother—coming to your fine house, Capel Carruthers, like a thief or a spy; slinking in at your gates, under cover of your fine friends' fine carriages; a prodigal step-son, by Jove, without the faintest chance of a welcome, and every probability of being turned out, if discovered. Company here, too, of all nights in the year, to make it more difficult to get hold of old Brookes unsuspected, but not so unfortunate either, if I'm seen. Hangers about are to be found even in the country, I suppose, on festive occasions. There's the house at last! A grand place, grim as it is under the stars, with a twinkling firmament of its own on the ground floor. The lights look warm. Good God, how cold it is out here!" Again he drew back close to the tall dark stems of the trees, to let a carriage pass; when it had discharged its load under the portico, he emerged cautiously upon the broad carriage sweep by which the company were arriving.

The house was an old one, and was surrounded by a narrow fosse or ditch, which in former days might have been full of water, and used for defensive purposes, but which was now drained and dry, and served as a kind of area, looked into by the windows in the basement. Above this fosse, and stretching away on either side of the heavy portico, was a broad and handsome stone terrace, the left hand portion of which lay in deep shadow, while the right hand portion was chequered with occasional light, which made its way through the partially closed shutters of the ball-room. Cautiously crossing the broad drive, and slipping behind a carriage which was just discharging its load at the hall door, George Dallas, the stranger whose fortunes we have so far followed, crept into a dark angle of the porch until the crunching of the gravel and the clanging of the door announced the departure of the carriage, and then, climbing the balustrade of the terrace, and carefully avoiding

the lines of light, made his way to the window of
the room, and peered in. At first, he shook so with
the cold, that he could not concentrate his attention
on what was passing before his eyes ; but having
groped about and found a small tree which was
carefully protected with a large piece of matting,
and which flanked one end of the balustrade, he
quietly removed the matting, and, wrapping it
round him, returned to his position, watching and
commenting on the scene of which he was a spectator.

It was an old room on which George Dallas
looked—an old room with panelled walls, sur-
mounted by a curious carved frieze and stuccoed
roof, and hung round with family portraits, which
gave it a certain grim and stern air, and made the
gay hothouse flowers, with which it was lavishly
decorated, seem out of keeping. Immediately opposite the window stood the entrance door, wide
open, and flanked by the usual bevy of young men,
who, from laziness or bashfulness, take some time
to screw their courage up to dancing-point. Close
in front of them was a group which at once arrested
George Dallas's attention.

It consisted of three persons, of whom two were gentlemen; the third was a young girl, whose small white-gloved hand rested on the arm of the older of her companions, who, as George Dallas caught sight of them, was in the act of presenting the younger to her. The girl was tall, slight, very graceful and elegant, and extremely fair. Her features were not clearly discernible, as she stood sideways towards the window; but the pose of the head, the bend of the neck, the braids of fair hair closely wound around the well-shaped head, and worn without any ornament but its own golden gloss, the sweeping folds of her soft white dress— all bore a promise of beauty, which indeed, her face, had he seen it, would have fully realised. He saw her bow, in graceful acknowledgment of the introduction, and then linger for a few minutes talking with the two gentlemen—to the younger of whom George Dallas paid no attention whatever; after which she moved away with him to join the dancers. The older man stood where she had left him, and at him George Dallas looked with the fixed intensity of anger and hatred.

"There you are," he muttered, "you worthy,

respectable, hard-hearted, unblemished gentleman !
There you are, with your clear complexion and
your iron-grey whiskers, with your cold blue eyes
and your white teeth, with your thin lips and your
long chin, with your head just a little bald, and
your ears just a little shrivelled, but not much ;
with your upright figure, and your nice cool hands,
and your nice cool heart, too, that never knew an
ungratified lust, or a passion which wasn't purely
selfish. There you are, the model of respectability
and wealth, and the essence of tyranny and pride !
There you are—and you married my beautiful
mother when she was poor, and when her son needed
all that she could give him, and more ; and you
gave her wealth, and a fine house, and fine friends,
and your not remarkably illustrious name, and
everything she could possibly desire, except the
only thing she wanted, and the only thing, as I
believe, for which she married you. That's your
niece, of course, the precious heiress, the rich and
rare young lady who has a place in your house,
though the son of its mistress is banished from it.
That's the heiress, who probably does not know
that I exist. I should not be surprised if he had

ordered my mother to conceal the disgraceful fact. Well, the girl is a nice creature, I dare say; she looks like it. But where can my mother be?"

He approached the window still more closely; he ventured to place his face close to the panes for a moment, as he peered anxiously into the room. "Where is my mother?" he thought. "Good Heaven! if she did but know that I am shivering here."

The strains of sweet clear music reached his ears, floods of light streamed out from the ball-room, a throng of dancers whirled past the window, he saw the soft fluttering dresses, he heard the rustle of the robes, the sounds of the gay voices, and the ring of laughter, and ever and anon, as a stray couple fell away from the dance, and lingered near the window, a fair young face would meet his gaze, and the happy light of its youth and pleasure would shine upon him. He lingered, fascinated, in spite of the cold, the misery of his situation, and the imminent risk of detection to which he was exposed. He lingered, and looked, with the long-ing of youth, for gaiety and pleasure; in his case for a simple gaiety, a more sinless pleasure, than any he was wont to know. Suddenly he shrank quickly back and clutched hard at the covering of matting in which he had shrouded himself. A figure had crossed the window, between him and the light—a figure he knew well, and recognised with a beating heart—a figure clad in purple velvet and decked with gleaming jewels; it was his mother. She passed hastily, and went up to Mr. Carruthers, then talking with another gentleman. She stretched out one jewelled arm, and touched him on the shoulder with her fan. Mr. Carruthers turned, and directly faced the window. Then George Dallas flung the matting which had covered him away, and left his hiding-place with a curse in his heart and on his lips.

"Yes, curse you," he said, "you dress her in velvet and diamonds, and make her splendid to entertain your company and flatter your pride, and you condemn her to such misery as only soft-hearted, strong-natured women such as she is can feel, all the time. But it won't do, Carruthers; she's my mother, though she's your wife, and you can't change her. I'll have some of your money, tyrant as you are, and slave as she is, before this night is over. I'm a desperate man; you can't make me more miserable than I am, and I *can* bring you to shame, and I *will*, too."

He stepped softly to the edge of the terrace, climbed the balustrade, and sat down cautiously on the narrow strip of grass beyond; then felt with his hands along the rough face of the wall which formed the front of the area. He looked down between his feet, the depth was about ten feet. He thought he might venture to let himself drop. He did so, and came safely on his feet, on the smooth sanded ground. An angle of the house was close to him; he turned it, and came upon a window whose shutters, like those of the upper range, were unclosed, and through which he could see into the comfortable room beyond. The room was low but large, and the heavy carved presses, the table with green baize cover, the arm-chairs, one at each side of the fire, the serviceable comfortable and responsible appearance of the apartment, at once indicated its true character. It could be nothing but the housekeeper's room.

In the centre of the table stood an old-fashioned oil-lamp, no doubt banished from the upper regions when the moderator made its appearance in society; close to the stand was a large Bible open, a pair of spectacles lying upon the page. A brass-bound desk, a file of receipts, a Tunbridge-ware workbox, and a venerable inkstand, were also symmetrically arranged upon the table. The room was empty, and the observer at the window had ample leisure and opportunity to scrutinise it.

"I am in luck," he said. "This is Nurse Ellen's room. There are the dreadful old portraits which she always insisted on keeping over the chimney-piece, and venerated, quite as much because she thought them objects of art, as because she fancied them really like my father and mother. There's her Bible, with the date of my birth and christening in it. I dare say those are the identical spectacles which I broke, playing Red Riding Hood's grand-mother. I wish she would come in, and come alone. What shall I do if she brings any one with her, and they close the shutters? How delightful the fire looks! I have a great mind to smash the window and get in. No one would hear the noise with all that crashing music overhead, and there does not seem to be a soul on this side of the house."

No sound of footsteps made itself audible on the terrace above his head. He was sheltered a little more in his present position, but still the cold was bitter, and he was shivering. The impulse to break the window grew stronger. He thought how he should avoid cutting his hand; his shabby gloves could not protect him, suppose he were to take off his waistcoat, and twist it around his hand and arm. He had unfastened one button of his coat, as the idea occurred to him, when a sound overhead, on the house side, caught his ear. It was the click produced by opening the fastening of a French window. Then came steps upon the light balcony, which was one of the modern decorations of the old building, and voices which reached him distinctly.

" Any influenza you may catch, or anything of that kind, you must ascribe to yourself, Miss Carruthers. You would come out this—hum—by Jove—awful night !"

" Oh, don't fear for me, Captain Marsh," said a light girlish voice, laughingly, "I'm country bred, you know, and accustomed to be out in all weathers, so that I run no risk; and though it is

wintry enough outside, the temperature of that
room was becoming unbearable !"

"Think it must be caused by that old woman's
red face that we noticed, or the thingummy—para-
dise feather in her cap. She with the very thin
daughter. Don't you know ?"

"Of course I know. The old lady is my
aunt, Lady Boldero ; the young one is my cousin
Blanche !"

"Haw, by Jove, sorry I spoke, haw ! By-the-
by, that was Sir Thomas Boldero's park, where I
met you riding on Friday, wasn't it, Miss Carruthers ?"

"Yes. I was taking a short cut home, as I
thought I should be late for dinner."

"You were going a rattling good pace, I
noticed. Seemed quite to have distanced your
groom."

"My groom ! That's a luxury I very seldom
indulge in—never, when I think I can dispense
with it without my uncle's knowledge. It is dis-
agreeable to me to have a man perpetually at my
heels !"

"You shouldn't say that, Miss Carruthers—

shouldn't, indeed. You don't know how pleasant it is—for the man."

"Very pretty indeed, Captain Marsh! And now that you've had the chance of paying a compliment, and have done it so neatly, we will go back, please. I begin to feel a little chilly."

As the speakers moved, something fell at George Dallas's feet. It was so dark in the corner where he stood, that he could not distinguish what it was, until the closing of the window above, gave him assurance that he might move in safety. Then he bent forward, and found it was a sprig of myrtle. He picked it up, looked at it idly, and put it into the breast-pocket of his coat.

"What a sweet voice she has!" he thought. "A sweet face too, I am sure; it must be so, to match the voice and the hair. Well, she has given me something, though she didn't intend it, and will probably never know it. A spirited, plucky girl, I am sure, for all her grace and her blonde style. Carries too many guns for the captain that's clear!"

He dived down in the midst of his thoughts, for the door of the room into which he had been looking, opened quietly, and an elderly woman in a black silk dress entered. After casting a glance round her, she was about to seat herself at the table, when Dallas gave two low taps in quick succession at the window. The woman started and looked towards the spot whence the sound came with a half-keen, half-frightened glance, which melted into unmixed astonishment when Dallas placed his face close to the glass and beckoned to her with his hand. Then she approached the window, shading her eyes from the candlelight and peering straight before her. When she was close to the window, she said, in a low firm voice:

"Who are you? Speak at once, or I'll call for help!"

"It's I, Nurse Ellen. I——"

"Good Heavens, Master George!"

"Yes, yes; open the window and let me in. I want to talk to you, and I'm half dead with cold. Let me in. So. That's it."

The woman gently raised the sash, and so soon as the aperture admitted of the passage of his body, he slipped through and entered the room, taking no notice of his old nurse, but making straight for the fire, before which he knelt, gazing hungrily at the flames, and spreading both his hands in eager welcome of the blaze. The old woman closed the window and then came softly behind him, placed her hand on his head, and, leaning over his shoulder and looking into his face, muttered : " Good Lord, how changed you are, my boy! I should scarcely have known you, except for your eyes, and they're just the same; but in every-thing else, how changed!"

He was changed indeed. The last time George Dallas had taken farewell of his old nurse, he had parted from her, a big strong healthy youth of eighteen, with short curly brown hair, clear skin, bright complexion, the incarnation of youth and strength and health. He knelt before her now, a gaunt grisly man, with high cheek-bones and hol-low rings round his great brown eyes, with that dead sodden pallor which a life of London dissi-pation always produces, and with long thin bony hands with which he clutched hold of the old woman, who put her arms round him and seemed about to burst into a fit of sobbing.

" Don't do that, nurse! don't do that! I'm

weak myself, and seedy, and couldn't stand it. Get me something to drink, will you? And, look here! I must see my mother to-night, at once. I've come from town on purpose, and I must see her."

"She does not know you are here?" asked Mrs. Brookes, while she gazed mournfully at the young man, still kneeling before the fire. "But of course she does not, or she would have told me."

"Of course, of course, Nurse Ellen," said George Dallas; "she knows nothing about it. If I had asked her leave, she would not have dared to give it. How is she, nurse? How does she like her life? She tells me very little of herself when she writes to me, and that's not often." He rose from his knees now, and pulled a ponderous black horsehair chair close to the fire, seated himself in it, and sat huddled together, as though cold even yet, with his feet on the broad old-fashioned fender. "I had to come at any risk. You shall know all about it, nurse; but now you must contrive to tell my mother I am here."

"How can I do that, Master George?" asked the old woman, in a tone of distress and perplexity.

"She is in the ball-room, and all the grand folk are looking at her and talking to her. I can't go in among them, and if I could, she would be so frightened and put about, that master would see in a moment that something had happened. He is never far off where she is."

"Ha!" said George gloomily; "watches her, does he, and that kind of thing?"

"Well, not exactly," said Mrs. Brookes ; "not in a nasty sort of way. I must say, to do him justice, though I don't much like him, that Mr. Carruthers is a good husband; he's fond of her, and proud of her, and he likes to see her admired."

The young man interrupted her with selfish heedlessness.

"Well, it's a pity he has the chance to-night; but, however it's managed, I must see her. I have to go back to town to-morrow, and of course I can't come about here safely in the daytime. Think of some plan, nurse, and look sharp about it."

"I might go upstairs and join the servants— they are all about the ball-room door—and watch for an opportunity as she passes."

"That will take time," said George, "but it's

the best chance. Then do it, nurse, and give me
something to eat while you are away. Will any
of the servants come in here? They had better
not see me, you know."

"No, you are quite safe; they are looking at
the dancing," she answered, absently, and closing
as she spoke the shutters of the window by which
he had entered. She then left the room, but
quickly returned, bringing in a tray with cold
meat, bread, and wine. He still sat by the fire,
now with his head thrown back against the high
straight back of his chair, and his hands thrust
into his pockets.

"Very plain fare, Master George," said the
housekeeper, "but I can't find anything better
without wasting time."

"Never mind, nurse. I'm not hungry, and
I'm not above eating cold meat if I were. Beg-
gars must not be choosers, you know; and I'm
little better than a beggar, as you also know.
Give me some wine. It isn't felony, is it, though I
have got into my step-father's house through the
window, and am drinking his wine without his
knowledge or consent ?"

His tone was very painful to the faithful old woman's ear. She looked at him wistfully, but made no reply. He rose from the chair by the fire, sullenly drew another chair to the table, and sat down by the tray. Mrs. Brookes left the room, and took her way along the white stone passage which led to the entrance hall of the mansion. Passing through a swinging door covered with crimson cloth, she entered a spacious square hall, decorated, after the fashion of country houses, with stags' heads and antlers. The floor was of polished oak, and uncarpeted, but at each of the six doors which opened into it lay a soft white rug. A bright fire blazed in the ample grate; and through the open door of the ball-room, light and the sound of music poured into the hall. A number of servants were standing about, some lingering by the fire, a few ranged close to the door of the dancing-room, exchanging comments upon the performances with perfect impunity. Under cover of the music Mrs. Brookes joined the group, which respectfully gave way at her approach, and ceded to her the front place. She looked anxiously, and for some time vainly, for her mistress. At length she perceived her, but she was seated at the further end of the room, in conversation with an elderly lady of extraordinary magnificence in point of apparel, and who required to be spoken to through an ear-trumpet. Mrs. Carruthers was not a skilful performer upon that instrument, and was obliged to give her whole mind to it, so that there was little chance of her looking in any other direction than the uninviting one of Mrs. Chittenden's ear for the present. Mrs. Brookes looked on impatiently, and longed for a break in the dancing, and a consequent movement among the company. At length the music ceased, the panting waltzers subsided into promenade, and Mrs. Carruthers rose to place her chair at the disposal of a young lady whose exertions had told upon her, and who breathlessly accepted the boon. As she stood for a moment turned towards the door, she caught sight of the housekeeper's face, and saw she looked pale and agitated. Catching her mistress's eye, the housekeeper made a slight stealthy sign. Very gracefully, and with perfect calm, the tall figure, in its sweeping velvet dress, made its way through the dispersed groups between it and the door, from which all the servants had precipitately retreated at the cessation of the music. What was wrong? Mrs. Carruthers thought. Something, she knew must be wrong, or Ellen would not be there beckoning to her. A second gesture, still more stealthy and warning, caused her to pause when within reach of the housekeeper's whisper, without turning her head towards her.

"What is it, Ellen?"

"Hush! where is master? Can he see you?"

"Yes, he is just beyond the screen. What is the matter?"

"Turn round, and stoop; let me tie your shoe —there!"

Mrs. Carruthers stood in the doorway, and bent her head, holding her foot out, and lifting her dress. Mrs. Brookes fumbled with the shoe, as she whispered rapidly:

"Come as soon as you can to my room. Be careful that you are not missed. Some one is there who wants to see you."

"To see me, Ellen? On such a night, and

at such an hour! What is wrong? Who is there?"

The old woman looked earnestly into the frightened face, bending over her, and said rather with her lips than with her voice: "Master George!"

CHAPTER II.

GEORGE DALLAS had eaten but sparingly of the food which Mrs. Brookes had placed before him. He was weary and excited, and he bore the delay and the solitude of the housekeeper's room with feverish impatience. He strode up and down the room, stopping occasionally before the fire to kick at the crumbling logs, and glance at the clock, which marked how rapidly the night was waning. Half an hour, which seemed three times as much to him, had elapsed since Mrs. Brookes had left him. Faintly and indistinctly the sounds of the music reached him, adding to his irritation and weariness. A savage frown darkened his face, and he muttered to himself in the same tone as that of his spasmodic soliloquy in the avenue :

" I wonder if she's thinking that I ought to be there too ; or if I ought not, neither ought she.

After all, I'm her son, and she might make a stand-up fight for me, if she would. He's fond of her, the old woman says, and proud of her, and well he may be. What's the use of it all, if she can't manage him? What fools women are! If they only could calculate at first, and take their own line from the beginning, they could manage any men. But she's afraid of him, and she lets him find it out. Well, well, it must be wretched enough for her, too. But why does she not come?"

He had to wait a little longer yet, for another quarter of an hour had elapsed before Mrs. Brookes returned.

"Is she coming?" he asked eagerly, when at length the pale-faced little woman gently entered the room.

"Yes, she is coming. She has to wait until the first lot are gone in to supper. Then master will not miss her."

The old woman came up to him, and took his right hand in hers, looking fondly, but keenly, into his face, and laying the other hand upon his shoulder. "George," she said, "George, my darling boy, I hope you have not brought her very bad news."

He tried to laugh as he loosed his hand, not unkindly, from the old woman's grasp.

"Do you suppose good news would have brought me here where I am forbidden—smuggled goods?"

She shook her head sorrowfully.

"At all events, you are alive and well to tell your ill news yourself, and that is everything to her," said Mrs. Brookes.

The next moment the door opened, and Mrs. Carruthers came in with a hurried step. George Dallas started forward, and caught her in his arms.

"Mother! mother!" "My boy, my darling boy!" were the only words spoken between them, until they were quite alone.

Mrs. Brookes left the room, and the young man was free to explain his untimely visit.

"I dread to ask what brings you here, George," said his mother, as she seated herself upon the heavy sofa, and drew him to her side. "I cannot but rejoice to see you, but I am afraid to ask you why you come."

A mingling of pleasure and apprehension shook her voice, and heightened her colour.

"You may well dread to ask me, mother," replied the young man, gloomily. "You may well dread to ask what brings me, outcast as I am, to your fine home, to the place where your husband is master, and where my presence is forbidden."

"George, George!" said his mother, in a tone of grief and remonstrance.

"Well, I know it's no fault of yours, but it's hard to bear for all that, and I'm not quite such a monster as I am made out to be, to suit Mr. Carruthers's purposes. I'm not so very much worse than the young men, mother, whose step-fathers, or whose own fathers either, don't find it necessary to forbid them the house. But you're afraid of him, mother, and—"

"George," said Mrs. Carruthers quietly, but sternly, "you did not come here to see me for the first time in nine months, at the risk of being turned out of Mr. Carruthers's house, simply to vent your anger upon him, and to accuse me wrongfully, and taunt me with what I am powerless to prevent. Tell me what has brought you here. I can stay with you only a little while; at any moment I may be missed. Tell me what has brought you against my husband's commands, contrary to my own entreaties, though it is such a delight to me to see you even 'so." And the mother put her arms around the neck of her prodigal son, and kissed him fondly. Her tears were falling on his rough brown curls.

"Don't cry over me, mother; I'm not worth it; I never was; and you mustn't go back to your company with pale cheeks and red eyes. There, there, it's not as bad as it might be, you know; for, as nurse says, I'm alive and well to tell it. The fact is—" He rose, and walked up and down the room in front of the sofa on which his mother was sitting, while he spoke. "The fact is, I must have money. Don't start, don't be frightened. I have not done anything very dreadful, only the consequences are nearly as fatal as if I had. I have not stolen, or forged, or embezzled property. I am not rich or respectable enough to get the chance. But I have lost a large sum at the gaming-table—a sum I don't possess, and have no other means than this of getting."

"Go on," said his mother. She was deadly pale now, and her hands were tightly clasped together, as they lay on her lap, white and slender, against the rich purple of her velvet dress.

He glanced at her, quickened his step, and continued in a hard reckless tone, but with some difficulty of utterance. "I should have been utterly ruined, but for a friend of mine, who lent me the money. Play debts must be paid, mother; and Routh, though he's not much richer than I am, would not let me be completely lost for want of a helping hand. But he had to borrow the money. He could get it lent to him. There's no one but him to lend *me* a shilling, and he did get it, and I had it and paid it away. But in a short time now he must pay it back and the interest upon it. Luck has been against us both."

"Against you *both*, George," said Mrs. Carruthers. "Is your friend also a gambler, then?"

"Yes, he is," said Dallas, roughly; "he is a gambler. All my friends are gamblers and drunkards, and everything that's bad. What would you have? Where am I to get pious, virtuous, respectable friends? I haven't a shilling; I haven't a character. Your husband has taken care I shall have no credit. Every one knows I am disowned by Mr. Carruthers, and forbidden to show my face at Poynings; and I'm not showing it; I'm only in the servants' quarters, you see." Again he laughed, and again his mother shrank from the sound. "But though my friend is a gambler, like myself, he helps me when I want help, and inconveniences himself to do it. Perhaps that's more than respectable friends—if I had them—would do for me. It's more than I have ever known respectable friends do for any one."

Mrs. Carruthers rose, and turned her colourless face upon her son. There was an angry light in her large hazel eyes, whose dewy brightness time had not yet greatly harmed. As they confronted each other, a strong likeness between the mother and son asserted itself. "George," she said, "you are putting me to needless pain. You have said enough to show me that you are unchanged. You have come here, endangering my peace, and compromising yourself, for the purpose, I suppose, of asking me for money to repay this person who re-

lieved you from a gambling debt. Is this your
business here?"

"Yes," he said shortly, and with a lowering brow.

"Then listen to me. I cannot give you any
money." He started, and came close up to her.
"No, George. I have no money at my disposal,
and you ought to know that, as well as I know it.
Every shilling I have ever had of my own, I have
given you. You know I never grudged it. You
know you had it all; but that leaves me without
resources. Mr. Carruthers will not help you." She
grew paler still, and her lips trembled. "I have
asked him many times to alter his determination, a
determination which you cannot say is undeserved,
George, but it is in vain. I might, perhaps, wonder that you would stoop to take assistance from a
man who has such an opinion of you, and who has
forbidden you his house, but that the sad knowledge I have gained of such lives as yours has
taught me that they utterly destroy self-respect—
that a profligate is the meanest of creatures. Calm
yourself. There is no use in giving loose to your
temper towards me, George. You have the power
to afflict me still, but you can deceive me no more."

She sat down again, wearily, leaning her arm on the back of the sofa, and her head on her hand. There was silence for a few moments. Then she said:

"How much money do you owe this man, George, and when must it be paid?"

"I owe him a hundred and forty pounds, mother, and it must be paid this day month."

"A hundred and forty pounds!" repeated Mrs. Carruthers, in a terrified tone.

"Yes; precisely that sum, and I have not a pound in the world to exist on in the mean time. I am cleaned out, that's the fact," he went on, with a dismal attempt at speaking lightly; "and I can't carry on any longer." But he spoke to inattentive ears. His mother was lost in thought.

"I cannot give you money," she said at length. "I have not the command of any."

"This doesn't look like want of it," said her son bitterly, as he caught a handful of her velvet dress in his grasp, and then dropped it scornfully.

"My personal expenses are all dictated by Mr. Carruthers, George, and all known to him. Don't suppose I am free to purchase dress or not, as I

choose. I tell you the exact truth, as I have always told you." She spoke coldly and seriously,
like one whose mind is made up to a great trial,
who hopes neither to alter its character nor to
lessen its weight.

"I only know I must have it," he said; "or I
don't see any resource for me except to cut my
throat."

"No, no," returned his mother, "do not say
such dreadful things. Give me time. I will try
to find some way of helping you by the time you
must have the money. O my boy, my boy!" she
covered her face with her hands and sobbed.

George Dallas looked at her irresolutely, then
came quickly towards her, and leaned over her,
as she sat. "Mother," he said, in low hurried
tones, "mother, trust me once more, little as I
deserve it. Try to help me in this matter; it is
life or death to me; and I will try and do better.
I am sick of it all; sick of my own weakness
above and more than all. But I am irretrievably
ruined if I don't get this money. I am quite in
Routh's power—and—and—I want to get out of
it."

She looked up curiously at him. Something in the way he said those words at once alarmed and reassured her.

"In this man's power, George? How? To what extent?"

"I cannot tell you, mother; you would not understand. Don't frighten yourself about it. It is nothing that money cannot settle. I have had a lesson now. You shake your head—well, I know I have had many before, but I *will* learn from this one."

"I have not the money, George," his mother repeated, "and I cannot possibly procure it for a little time. You must not stay here."

"I know, I know," he retorted. "You need not re-echo Mr. Carruthers's interdict. I am going; but surely you can give me a little now; the price of one of these things would go a long way with me." As he spoke, he touched, but with no rough hand, her earrings and the bracelet on her right arm.

"They are family jewels, or you should have them, George," Mrs. Carruthers said, in a sad voice. "Give me time, and I will make up the

money for you. I have a little I can give you."
She stood up and looked fixedly at him, her hands
resting on his shoulder. The tall and powerful
young man, with his haggard anxious face, his
hardened look, his shabby careless dress, offered
a strange contrast to the woman, whose beauty
time had dealt with so lightly, and fortune so
generously. Mrs. Carruthers had been a mere
girl when her son was born, and probably had
not been nearly so beautiful as now, when the
calm dignity of position and the power of wealth
lent all their attractions to her perfect face and
form.

The habitual seriousness of her expression was
but a charm the more, and in moments of excited feeling like the present she regained the lus-
trous brilliancy of the past. Searchingly, fondly,
she gazed into her son's face, as though reading
it for traces of the truth of his promises, seeing
in it but too surely indications of the weary, un-
satisfying life he had led, the life which had
brought disappointment to all her dearest maternal hopes. Steadily and tenderly he looked at
her, a world of regret in his eyes. While they

stood thus in brief silence, Mrs. Brookes came in hurriedly.

"You are wanted," she said. "Master is asking for you; he has sent Miss Clare to your room to see if you are ill."

"I must go, my boy," said Mrs. Carruthers, as she hastily kissed him; "and you must not stay. Come with me, Ellen, for a moment. Wait here, George, for what I promised you, and don't travel back to town without an overcoat." Then she left the room at once, the housekeeper with her. George stood where she had left him, looking towards the door.

"My dear practical mother," he said to himself, "she is as kind and as sensible as ever. Wretched about me, but remembering to desire me to buy a coat! I know she will get me the money somehow, and this *shall* be the last scrape I will get into. It's no use being melodramatic, especially when one is all alone, but I here make a solemn promise to myself that I will keep my promise to *her*."

He sat down by the fire, and remained still and thoughtful. In a few minutes Mrs. Brookes returned.

"Here's the money, Master George," she said. "I was to give it to you with my mistress's love, and she will write to you to London."

He took the folded paper from her hand. It was a ten-pound note.

"Thank you, nurse," he said; "and now I will go. I would like to stay and have a talk with you; but I had better get away, lest any annoyance should come to my mother through my staying. I'll see you when you come up to town to the fine house in Mesopotamia. Eh?"

"Lord, Master George, how you do go on! Why, Mr. Carruthers's new house is the far side of the Park."

"I know, nurse. It's all the same thing. No. No more wine, thank you, and nothing to eat. Good-bye.—How am I to get out, though? Not through the window, and up the area wall, am I?"

"I'll show you, Master George. This way."

George Dallas buttoned his coat tightly across his breast, carefully put on his gloves, and took up his hat. As he followed Mrs. Brookes through the long stone passages of the basement story, he looked curiously about him, noting the details of comfort and convenience. "How much better off than I are my mother's servants!" he thought, idly rather than bitterly. When they reached a door which opened upon the court-yard, Mrs. Brookes bade him farewell, not without emotion.

"The great gates are open," she said. "All the servants are either in the hall or the servants' hall. None of the carriages have been called yet. You can slip past without being seen; or if any one sees you, they'll think you belong to the place."

"A serious mistake, dear old woman," said George, with a half smile, as he once more shook her hand, and stepped out into the cold and darkness. A bitter sense of desolation came over him as the door closed behind him. The court-yard was empty, except of carriages, and he crossed it quickly, and went through the great gates into the avenue, which swept round the terrace. Following it, he found himself brought again by a different route in front of the lighted ball-room; but he did not delay to glance at the scene.

"So I am going away," he said to himself, "richer by ten pounds and my mother's promise.

Stop, though! There's the sprig of myrtle. I must not forget or lose the unconscious gift of the great heiress. I wish I had asked nurse what sort of girl she is. I might have taken time to do that. It's not so cold as it was." He had been warmed and fed, and his spirits had risen. It did not take much to raise George Dallas's spirits, even now when the excesses of his wasted life were beginning to tell upon him. "I feel quite strong again. The night is lighter; the village must be a wretched place. I have a great mind to push on to Amherst. It's only seven miles, and Carruthers can't hear that I have been there; but he might hear of me at the village, and bother my mother about it."

He took his way down the avenue and reached the gate, which lay open. One feeble light twinkled from the upper window of the gate lodge. Bulger and family had retired to rest, the excitement of the arrivals being over; and Bulger would leave the gate to take care of itself until morning. Unquestioned, unseen, George Dallas left Poynings, and, turning to the right under the park wall, set forth at a steady pace towards Amherst.

The town of Amherst is very much like the other towns in that part of the country. Close by the railway station lies the Railway Tavern, snug and comfortable, with a "quick draught" of home-brewed ale and bitter beer, thanks to the powers of suction of porters, guards, and admiring friends of both, who vent their admiration in "standing glasses round." Not a little of its custom does the Railway Tavern owe to that small plot of waste ground in front of it, where, even on this desolate night, you might trace the magic circle left by the "ring" of Signor Quagliasco's Mammoth Circus on its visit last autumn, and the holes for the pole and tent-pegs, and the most recent ruts on which were left by the wheels of the cart of the travelling photographer who "took" the entire town at Christmas, and, in addition to the photograph, presented each sitter with a blue card embossed with a scarlet robin bearing in its mouth the legend, "A happy new year to you." Then villas; Mr. Cobb's, the corn-chandler and coal-merchant, with a speckled imitation-granite porch, white and black, as if it had been daubed with a mixture of its owner's flour and coal-dust;

Mr. Lawson's, the attorney, with a big brass plate
on its outer gate, and two stone pine-apples flank-
ing the entrance; Mr. Charlton Biggs's, the hop-
merchant, in all the gentility of a little chaise-
house leaning against the street door, approached
by a little carriage-drive so narrow that the pony
had never yet walked up it properly, but had always been ignominiously "backed" into its tiny
home. Then the outskirts of the town; the Independent Chapel, very square, very red-faced, and
very compact, not to say sat upon; the Literary
Institute, with more green damp on its stuccoed
walls than had been originally intended by its
architect, and with fragmentary bills of " Mr.
Lens's Starry Carpet, or the Heavens . at a
Glance," fluttering in the night wind from its
portico. Merton House comes next, formerly the
stronghold of the Merton-Mertons, the great Kentish family, now Mr. Bompas's Classical and Com-
mercial Academy, with a full view of the white
dimity bedsteads through the open window, and
with " Old Bompas's Blaggards" inscribed—by the
boys of the National School, with whom the grand
Bompasians waged constant warfare—on the door-

post. The commencement of the town, a mouldy old bay-windowed shop, known to Mr. Bompas's boys as " Mother Jennings's," and as the repository of " tuck," said tuck consisting of stale buns, hardbake, " all sorts," toffee, treacle, new rolls, sugar mutton-chops elegantly painted and gilt, sugar rum and gin bottles, whipcord, pegtops, and marbles; then Bullenger's, apparently a small ironmonger's, but in reality another lure for the money of Bompas's boys, for in a parlour behind his back shop Bullenger vended fireworks and half-crown detonating pistols, catapults, and cross-bows, and all sorts of such-like instruments dear to predatory boys. Then the ordinary lot of butchers, bakers, tailors, hosiers, grocers, chemists (Mr. Hotten, member of the Pharmaceutical Society of Great Britain, also strongly reliant on Bompas's custom for cigars and hair-oil for the big boys, and bath-pipe and liquorice for the little ones), and then the police-station; the old gray church, with its square ivy-covered tower, its billowy graves and its half-obliterated sun-dial over the porch, and then the fresh green fields again.

All these particulars George Dallas noted in the morning, when, having early left the bed he had procured at the inn, he called in at the station and learned from the friendly porter, who was again engaged in mending his shoes with tin and tacks, when the next train would start for London, and where he could find a tailor's shop, walked briskly through the little town, with feelings very different from those which had possessed him on his first arrival at the Amherst station. Now, his step was free and light, he carried his head erect, and though he occasionally shivered as the cold wind came sweeping over the downs and gave him a sharp unfriendly nip as it hurried by him in its progress to the sea, he bore the insult with tolerable fortitude, and seemed to derive immediate comfort from plunging his hand into his trousers-pocket, where lay the ten-pound note he had received from his mother. It was there, stiff and crisp to his touch. He had taken it out and looked at it twice or thrice on the road, but he could not do that now in the town ; he must content himself with touching it, and the crinkling sound was music in his ear; he had been so long

without money, that he derived the keenest pleasure from the possession of this actual tangible
sum, and felt so little inclined to part with it, that,
though he had passed, and noticed in passing, the
tailor's shop to which he had been recommended
by the porter, he still walked on. It was not
until he had made a circuit of the old churchyard
at the end of the town, where even on summer
days the wind is generally at play, and where on
winter nights it ramps and rages in a manner
terrible to hear and feel, that George Dallas began
to comprehend the necessity of at once procuring
some warmer clothing, and, turning back, made
straight for the tailor's shop.

A neat, clean-looking shop, with " Evans,
Tailor," painted over the window, the effect being
slightly spoiled by the knob of the roller blind,
which formed a kind of full-stop in the middle of
the word " Tail. or," and divided it into two un-
equal portions; with "Evans, Tailor," blazing from
its brass door-plate; with "Evans, Tailor," inscribed with many twisted flourishes on its wire
blind, where it emerged coyly from " Liveries"
preceding it, and took hasty refuge in " Uniforms"

at its conclusion.   Evans himself behind the coun-
ter, a fat, chubby, rosy little man, with clustering
iron-gray hair round his temples, and a bit of
round scalp wig fitting, like the lid of a teapot,
into a bald place on his crown.   Apparently he
had been all his life tailoring to such an extent
for other people as to have had no time to attend
to himself, for he stood behind the counter this
winter's day in his shirt-sleeves, and without his
coat.

The old man bowed as George Dallas entered
the shop, and asked him what they could do for
him.   Dallas replied that he wanted a warm thick
overcoat, "if they'd got such a thing."

"Such a thing!   Well, there may be such a
thing, perhaps, but I'm not certain, not being an
article kept in stock," replied Mr. Evans, "which
is mostly tarpaulin for the railway guards and
stokers, likewise canal boatmen, which is often
customers.   A warm thick overcoat," repeated
the old man, "is a article generally made to order,
though I've a sort of a recollection of a something
of the kind returned on our hands in consequence
of the party which was staying at the Lion having

left unexpected. Let me see!" he continued, opening two or three drawers. "I ain't so young as I was, sir, and I'm touched in the wind; and this nasty gas which we've only had this winter don't do for me, making me bust out in sudden presperation. Ho! I thought so! Here's a warm thick overcoat, blue Witney, lined with plaid; that's a article I can recommend; our own make; we ain't ashamed of it, you see!" and he pointed to a label stitched inside just below the collar, where the inevitable "Evans, Tailor," in gilt letters, was supplemented by the address, "Amherst."

George Dallas took the coat and slipped it on. It fitted tolerably, and was thick and warm. "What is the price?" he asked.

"We can do that for you at fifty-three and six," said the old man. "It was a three-pounder, that coat was, when made for the party at the Lion, but we'll make a reduction now. Fifty-three and six, and our own make. You couldn't do better."

"I dare say not," said Dallas absently. "Please to change this for me."

At the sight of the bank-note Mr. Evans's pleasant face became a little clouded. He did not relish the notion of changing notes for persons with whom he had no previous acquaintance. But after he had taken the note in his hand and held it between his eyes and the light, and flattened it out on the counter, his cheerful expression returned, and he said, "All right, sir. I'll change it and welcome! I know where you got this note, sir! Ah, you may start, but I do! You got it from our post-office, lower down the street; here's the post-office stamp on it, which they're compelled to put on every note passing through their hands. Look, 'Amherst, B. 1, Jan. 30.' Thank you, sir; six and six's, three and seven is ten; thank you, sir!" and the old man, having counted the change from a cash-box in a desk at the back of the shop, hurried round to open the door and bow his customer out.

Within half an hour George Dallas was in the train on his return to London.

CHAPTER III.

THE cold weather, which in the country produced rugged roads and ice-bound ponds; which frosted the leafless branches of the trees with a silver tint, and gave a thousand different fantastic but ever lovely hues and shapes to nature; had no such pleasant refreshing effect in London, where the frost, ere three hours old, was beaten into mud under foot, ran drizzling in dirty streams from house-tops, and subsided into rain and fog before the daylight had disappeared. The day succeeding that on which George Dallas had entered the town of Amherst was a thorough specimen of what Lon-don can do when put to its worst. It was bad in the large thoroughfares where the passing crowds jostled each other ill-temperedly, digging at each other's umbrellas, and viciously contesting every inch of foot pavement, where the omnibus wheels

revolved amid mud-ruts, and every passing cab-
horse produced a fountain of slush and spray. But
it was even worse in the by-streets, where an
attempt at sweeping had been made, where the
mud lay in a thick slimy, shiny tide between the
narrow ridges of footpath, where the tall houses,
so close together that they completely filtered the
air and light and retained nothing but the darkness and the dirt, were splashed with mud to
their first-floor windows, and whose inhabitants or
visitors desirous of crossing the road had to proceed to the junction with the main street, and,
after tacking across in comparative cleanliness,
commence their descent on the opposite side.

In the front room of the first floor of a house
in such a street, South Molton-street, connecting
Oxford-street the plebeian with Brook-street the
superb, just as the feeble glimmer of daylight
which had vouchsafed itself during the day was
beginning to wax even feebler, previous to its sudden departure, a man sat astride a chair, sunk in
thought. He had apparently just entered, for he
still wore his hat and overcoat, though the former
was pushed to the back of his head, and the latter

thrown negligently open. He was a tall handsome man, with keen black eyes glancing sharply, with thick black brows, a long straight nose, thin tight lips unshrouded by moustache or beard, and a small round chin. He had full flowing black whiskers, and the blue line round his mouth showed that the beard was naturally strong; had he suffered it to grow, he might have passed for an Italian. As it was, there was no mistaking him for anything but an Englishman—darker, harder-looking than most of his race, but an Englishman. His face, especially round the eyes, was flushed and marked and lined, telling of reckless dissipation. There was a something not exactly fast, but yet slangy, in the cut of his clothes and in the manner in which he wore them; his attitude as he sat at the window with his hands clasped in front of him over the back rail of his chair, his knees straight out and his feet drawn back, as a man sits a horse at a hunt, was in its best aspect suggestive of the mess-room: in its worst, of the billiard-room. And yet there was an indescribable something in the general aspect of the man, in the very ease of his position, in the shape of the hands

58 BLACK SHEEP.

clasped in front of him, in the manner, slight as it
was, in which now and again he would turn on
his chair and peer back into the darkness behind
him, by which you would have known that he had
had a refined education, and had been conversant
with the manners of society.

Nor would you have been wrong. In Burke's
Landed Gentry, the Rouths of Carr Abbey take
up their full quota of pages, and when the county
election for Herefordshire comes off, the liberal
agent is forced to bring to bear all the science he
can boast of, to counteract the influence which the
never-failing adhesion of the old family throws
into the Tory scale. Never having risen, never
for an instant having dreamed of demeaning themselves by rising, above the squirearchy, owners
of the largest and best herds in all that splendid
cattle-breeding county, high-sheriffs and chairmen
of quarter-sessions as though by prescriptive right,
perpetual presidents of agricultural societies, and
in reality taking precedence immediately after the
lord-lieutenant, the Rouths of Carr Abbey, from
time immemorial, have sent their sons to Oxford and their daughters to court, and have

never, save in one instance, had to blush for their children.

Save in one instance. The last entry in the old family Bible of Carr Abbey is erased by a thick black line. The old squire speaks habitually of "My only son, William;" and should a stranger, dining at the Abbey, casually refer to the picture, by Lawrence, of two little boys, one riding a pony, the younger decking a dog's neck with ribbon, he is, if the squire has not heard his question, motioned in dumb show to silence, or is replied to by the squire himself that "that boy is—lost, sir."

That boy, Stewart Routh, the man looking out of the window in South Molton-street, was captain of the boat at Eton, and first favourite, for a time, both with the dons and undergraduates at Oxford. Rumours of high play at cards developing into fact of perpetually sported "oak," non-attendance at chapel, and frequent shirking of classes, lessened the esteem in which Mr. Routh was held by the authorities; and a written confession handed to the dean, after being obtained by parental pressure, from Mr. Albert Grüntz, of Christ Church, son of and heir to Mr. Jacob Grüntz, sugar-baker,

of St. Mary Axe, in the city of London, and Bal-
moral-gardens, Hyde-park, a confession to the
effect that he, Mr. A. Grüntz, had lost the sum
of two thousand pounds to Mr. S. Routh, at a
game played with dice, and known as French
hazard, procured the dismissal of Mr. S. Routh
from the seat of learning. At Carr Abbey, whither
he retired, his stay was shortened by the arrival of
another document from Oxford, this time signed by
Lord Hawkhurst, gentleman commoner of Christ
Church, and Arthur Wardroper, of Balliol, setting
forth that Mr. S. Routh, while playing hazard in
Mr. Grüntz's rooms, had been caught there *in
flagrante delicto* in the act of cheating by "securing," *i.e.* retaining in his fingers, one of the dice
which he should have shaken from the box. It
was the receipt of this letter that caused the squire
to make the erasure in the family Bible, and to
look upon his youngest son as dead.

Driven from the paternal roof, Mr. Stewart
Routh descended upon the pleasant town of Bou-
logne, whence, after a short stay not unmarked by
many victories over the old and young gentlemen
who frequent the card-tables at the Etablissement

des Bains, from whom he carried off desirable tro-
phies, he proceeded to the baths and gambling-
houses of Ems, Homburg, and Baden-Baden. It
was at the last-mentioned place, and when in the
very noon and full tide of success, that he was
struck down by a fever, so virulent that the
affrighted servants of the hotel refused to wait
upon him. No nurse could be prevailed upon to
undertake to attend him ; and he would have
been left to die for want of proper care, had not
a young Englishwoman, named Harriet Creswick,
travelling in the capacity of nursery-governess to
Lord de Mauleverer's family (then passing through
Baden on their way to winter in Rome), come to
the rescue. Declaring that her countryman should
not perish like a dog, she there and then devoted
herself to attendance on the sick man. It need
scarcely be told that Lady de Mauleverer, pro-
testing against " such extraordinary conduct," in-
timated to Miss Creswick that her connection with
her noble charges must cease at once and for ever.
But it is noteworthy that in such a man as Stewart
Routh had hitherto proved himself, a spirit of gratitude should have been so strongly aroused, that

when his sense and speech returned to him, in weak and faltering accents he implored the woman who had so tenderly nursed him through his illness, to become his wife. It is quite needless to say that his friends, on hearing of it, averred, some that he thought he was going to die, and that it did not matter to him what he did, while it might have pleased the young lady; others, that he was a particularly knowing card whose brains had never deserted him, even when he was at his worst, and that he had discovered in Harriet Creswick a woman exactly fitted, by physical and mental qualifications, efficiently to help him as his partner in playing the great game of life. Be it as it may—and people will talk, especially in such circles—the fact remains that on his sick couch at the Hollandischer Hof, Baden-Baden, Stewart Routh proposed to Harriet Creswick and was accepted; that so soon as he could safely be left, she departed for England ; and that within a month they were married in London.

Of that one event at least in all his eventful life, Stewart Routh had never repented. Through all his vicissitudes of fortune his wife had been by

his side, and, as in the long run, chance had been
against him, taking the heaviest portion of his
burden on herself. Harriet Routh's was an un-
tiring, undying, unquestioning love or worship of
her husband. The revelation of his—to say the
least of it—loose mode of life, the shifts and expedients to which he resorted for getting money,
the questionable company in which he habitually
lived, would have told with fatal effect on a devotion less thorough, a passion more transient.
Harriet herself, who had been brought up staidly
at an Institution, which she had only quitted to
join the family with whom she was travelling when
she arrived at Baden — Harriet herself at first
shrunk back stunned and stupefied by the reve-
lations of an unknown life which burst upon her a
few days after her marriage. But her love bore
her through it. As the dyer's hand assimilates to
that it works in, so gradually did Harriet Routh
endue herself with her husband's tone, temper,
and train of thought, until, having become almost
his second self, she was his most trusted ally, his
safest counsellor in all the strange schemes by
which he made out life. In the early days after

their marriage she had talked to him once, only
once, and then but for a few minutes, of reformation, of something better and more reputable, of
doing with less money, to be obtained by the exercise of his talents in some legitimate manner.
And her husband, with the nearest approach to
harshness that before or since he had ever assumed,
told her that his time for that kind of thing was
passed and gone for ever, that she must forget all
the childish romance that they had taught her ,
at the Institution, that she must sink or swim with
him, and be prepared to cast in her lot with that
kind of existence which had become his second
nature, and out of which he could never hope to
move.   Even if he could move from it, he added,
he did not think that he would wish to do so, and
there must be an end to the matter.

There was an end to the matter.   From that
time forth, Harriet Routh buried her past, buried
her former self, and devoted herself, soul and
body, to her husband.   Her influence over him
strengthened with each year that they lived
together, and was traceable in many ways.
The fact once faced, that their precarious liveli-

hood was to be earned by the exercise of sharp-
ness superior to that enjoyed by those with whom
they were brought into contact, Harriet laid herself out at once for the fulfilment of her new
duties, and in a very short time compelled her
husband's surprised laudation of the ease and coolness with which she discharged them. There
were no other women in that strange society;
but if there had been, Harriet would have queened
it over them, not merely by her beauty, but by
her bright spirit, her quick appreciation, her tho- ·
rough readiness to enter exactly into the fancy
of the moment. The men who lost their money
to Routh and his companion, treated her not
merely with a punctilio which forbade the smallest verbal excess, but bore their losses with
comparative good humour so long as Mrs. Routh
was present. The men who looked up to Routh
as the arch concoctor of and prime mover in all
their dark deeds, had a blind faith in her, and
their first question, on the suggestion of any
scheme, would be " what Mrs. Routh thought of
it." Ah, the change, the change! The favourite pupil of the Institution, who used to take such

close notes of the sermon on Sunday mornings, and illustrate the chaplain's meaning with such apposite texts from other portions of Scripture, as quite to astonish the chaplain himself, which perhaps was not to be wondered at, as the chaplain (a bibulous old gentleman, who had been appointed on the strength of his social qualities by the committee, who valued him as "a parson, you know, without any nonsense about him") was in the habit of purchasing his discourses ready made, and only just ran them through on Saturday nights. The show pupil of the Institution, who did all kinds of arithmetical problems "in her head," by which the worthy instructors meant without the aid of paper and pencil—the staid and decorous pupil of the Institution, who, when after her last examination she was quitting the table loaded with prizes—books—was called back by the bishop of the diocese, who with feeble hands pinned a silver medal on to her dress, and said, in a trembling voice, "I had nearly forgotten the best of all. This is in testimony of your excellent conduct, my dear." What was become of this model miss? She was utilising her talents

in a different way. That was all. The memory
which had enabled her to summarise and annotate
the chaplain's sermons now served as her husband's note-book, and was stored with all kinds
of odd information, "good things" to "come off,"
trials of horses, names and fortunes of heirs who
had just succeeded to their estates, lists of their
most pressing debts, names of the men who were
supposed to be doubtful in money matters, and
with whom it was thought inexpedient to bet or
play—all these matters dwelt in Harriet Routh's
brain, and her husband had only to turn his head
and ask, "What is it, Harry?" to have the information at once. The arithmetical quickness
stood her in good stead, in the calculation of odds
on all kinds of sporting events, on the clear knowledge of which the success of most of Routh's
business depended; and as for the good conduct
—well, the worthy bishop would have held up
his hands in pious horror at the life led by the
favourite pupil of the Institution, and at her surroundings; but against Mrs. Routh, as Mrs.
Routh, as the devoted, affectionate, self-denying, spotless wife, the veriest ribald in all that

loose crew had never ventured to breathe a
doubt.

Devoted and affectionate! See her now as
she comes quietly into the room—a small compact partridge of a woman with deep blue eyes
in a very pale face, with smooth shining light
brown hair falling on either side in two long curls,
and gathered into a clump at the back of her
head, with an impertinent nose only just redeemed
from being a snub, with a small mouth, and a
very provoking pattable chin. See how she steals
behind her husband, her dark linsey dress draping
her closely and easily, and not making the slightest rustle; her round arm showing its symmetry
in her tight sleeve twining round his neck; her
plump shapely hand resting on his head; her pale
cheek laid against his face. Devoted and affectionate! No simulation here.

"Anything gone wrong, Stewart?" she asked,
in a very sweet voice.

"No, dear. Why?" said Routh, who was now
sitting at a table strewn with papers, a pen in
his right hand, and his left supporting his handsome worn face.

"You looked gloomy, I thought; but, if you say so, it's all right," returned his wife, cheerfully, leaving his side as she spoke, and proceeding to sweep up the hearth, put on fresh coals, and make the whole room look comfortable, with a few rapid indefinable touches. Then she sat down in a low chair by the fire, perfectly still, and turned her calm pale face to her husband with a business-like air. He made some idle scratches with his pen in silence, then threw it down, and, suddenly pushing away his chair, began to walk up and down the room with long light strides.

"What do you make of Deane, Harriet?" he said, at length, stopping for a moment opposite his wife, and looking closely at her.

"How do you mean? In character or in probabilities? As regards himself, or as regards us?"

"Well, both. I cannot make him out; he is so confoundedly cool, and so infernally sharp. He might be a shrewd man of business, bent on making a fortune, and a good way on the road to his object; and yet he's nothing but a man of pleasure, of what your *good* people would call a wretched low kind of pleasure too, and is spending the fortune instead."

"I don't think so, Stewart," his wife said, quietly and impressively. "I don't think Mr. Deane is spending any very considerable portion of his fortune, whatever it may be."

Stewart had resumed his walking up and down, but listened to her attentively.

"I regard him as a curious combination of the man of business with the man of pleasure. I don't know that we have ever met exactly the kind of person before. He is as calculating in his pleasures as other men are in their business."

"I hate the man," said Routh, with an angry frown and a sullen gesture.

"That's dangerous, Stewart," said Harriet. "You should not allow yourself either to hate or to like anyone in whom you are speculating. If you do the one, it will make you incautious; if you do the other, scrupulous. Both are unwise. I do not hate Mr. Deane."

"Fortunately for him, Harry. I think a man would be a great deal safer with my hatred than with yours.'

" Possibly," she said, simply, and the slightest
smile just parted her crimson lips, and showed
a momentary gleam of her white, small, even
teeth. " But I do not hate him. I think about
him, though ; because it is necessary that I
should, and I fancy I have found out what he
really is."

" Have you, by Jove?" interrupted Routh.
" Then you've done a clever thing, Harriet—
clever even for you; for of all the close and im-
penetrable men I ever met, Deane's the closest
and the hardest. When I'm with him, I always
feel as if he were trying to *do* me somehow, and
as if he would succeed too, though that's not easy.
He's as mean as a Scotch shopkeeper, as covetous
as a Jew, as wide awake as a Yankee. There's
a coolness and a constant air of avowed suspicion
about him that drives me mad."

" And yet you ought to have been done with
temper and with squeamishness long ago," said
Harriet, in a tone of quiet conviction. " How
often have you told me, Stewart, that to us, in
our way of life, every man must be a puppet,
prized in proportion to the readiness with which

he dances to our pulling? What should *we* care? I am rendered anxious and uneasy by what you say."

She kept silence for a few moments, and then asked him, in a changed tone,

"How does your account with him stand?"

"My account!—ah, there's the rub! He's so uncommonly sharp, that there's little to be done with him. The fellow's a blackguard—more of a blackguard than I am, I'll swear, and as much of a swindler, at least, in his capacity for swindling. Only I dare say he has never had occasion to reduce it to practice. And yet there's a hardly veiled insolence in his manner to me, at times, for which I'd like to blow his brains out. He tells me, as plainly as if he said it in words, that he pays me a commission on his pleasures, such as are of my procuring, but that he knows to a penny what he intends to pay, and is not to be drawn into paying a penny more."

Harriet sat thoughtful, and the faintest flush just flickered on her check. "Who are his associates, when he is not with you?"

"He keeps that as close as he keeps everything else," replied Routh; "but I have no doubt he makes them come cheap, if indeed he does not get a profit out of them."

"You are taking my view of him, Stewart," said Harriet; then she added, "He has some motive for acting with such caution, no doubt; but a flaw may be found in his armour, when we think fit to look for it. In the mean time, tell me what has set you thinking of him?"

"Dallas's affair, Harriet. I am sorry the poor fellow lost his money to *him*. Hang it, I'm such a bad fellow myself, so utterly gone a 'coon" (his wife winced, and her pale face turned paler), "that it comes ill from me to say so, and I wouldn't, except to you. But I am devilish sorry Deane got the chance of cleaning Dallas out. I like the boy; he's a stupid fool, but not half bad, and he didn't deserve such an ill turn of fortune."

"Well," said Harriet, "take comfort in remembering that you helped him."

She spoke very coldly, and evidently was a stranger to the feelings which actuated Routh.

"*You* don't care about it, that's clear," he remarked.

He was standing still now, leaning against the mantelpiece. She rose and approached him.

"No, Stewart," she said, in her calm sweet voice, which rose a little as she went on, "I do not. I care for nothing on earth (and I never look beyond this earth) but *you*. I have no interest, no solicitude, for any other creature. I cannot feel any, and it is well. Nothing but this would do in my case."

She stood and looked at him with her deep blue eyes, with her hands folded before her, and with a sober seriousness in her face confirmatory of the words she had spoken. He looked at her until she turned away, and a keen observer might have seen in his face the very slightest expression of impatience.

"Shall we go into those accounts now?" said Harriet; "we shall just have time for it, before you go to Flinders'."

She sat down, as she spoke, before a well-appointed writing table, and, drawing a japan box towards her, opened it, and took out a number of papers. Routh took a seat beside her, and they were soon deep in calculations which would have had little interest or meaning for a third person, had there been one present. By degrees, Routh's face darkened, and many times he uttered angry oaths; but though Harriet watched him narrowly, and felt in every nerve the annoyance under which he was labouring, she preserved her calm manner, and went steadily on with her task; condensing the contents of several papers into brief memoranda, carefully tearing up the originals, and placing the little heaps methodically beside her for consignment to the fire. At length Routh again stood up, and lounged against the mantelpiece.

"All these *must* be paid, then, Harry?" he asked, as he lighted a cigar, and began to smoke sullenly.

"Yes," she answered, cheerfully. "You know, dear, it has always been our rule, as it has hitherto constituted our safety, to stand well with our tradespeople, and pay *them*, at least, punctually. We have never been so much behindhand; and as you are about to take a bolder flight than usual, it is doubly necessary that we should be untrammelled. Fancy Flinders getting snubbed by the landlady, or your being arrested for your tailor's bills, at the time when the new Company is coming out!"

"Hang it! the bills all seem to be mine," growled Routh. "Where are yours? Haven't you got any?"

It would have been difficult to induce an unseen witness to believe how utterly unscrupulous, remorseless, conscienceless a woman Harriet Routh had become, if he had seen the smile with which she answered her husband's half-admiring, half-querulous question.

"You know, dear, I don't need much. I have not to keep up appearances as you have. You are in the celebrated category of those who cannot afford to be anything but well-dressed. It's no matter for me, but it's a matter of business for you."

"Ah! I might have known you'd have some self-denying, sensible reason ready; but the puzzle to me is, that you always *are* well dressed. By Jove, you're the neatest woman I know, and the prettiest!"

The smile upon her face brightened, but she only shook her head, and went on:

" If Dallas does not get the money, or at least some of it, what do you propose to do ? I don't know."

" Do you think he will get the money, Harry ? He told *you* all about it. What are the odds ?"

" I cannot even guess. All depends on his mother. If she is courageous, and fond of him, she will get it for him, even supposing her immediate control as small as he believes it to be. If she is not courageous, her being fond of him will do very little good, and women are mostly cowards," said Harriet, composedly.

" I never calculated much on the chance," said Routh, " and indeed it would be foolish to take the money if he got it—in that way, at least ; for though I am sorry Deane profited by the young fellow, that's because I hate Deane. It's all right, for my purpose, that Dallas should be indebted as largely as may be to me. He's useful in more ways than one ; his connexion with the press serves our turn, Harry, doesn't it ? Especially when you work it so well, and give him such judicious hints, such precious confidences."

(Even such praise as this, the woman's perverted nature craved and prized.) "You won't
need to take the money from him in formal payment," she said, "if that's what you want to avoid.
If he returns with that sum in his pocket, he will
not be long before he—"

A knock at the door interrupted her, and
George Dallas entered the room.

He looked weary and dispirited, and, before
the customary greetings had been exchanged,
Routh and Harriet saw that failure had been the
result of experiment. Harriet's eyes sought her
husband's face, and read in it the extent of his dis-
comfiture; and the furtive glance she turned on
Dallas was full of resentment. But it found no
expression in her voice, as she asked him commonplace questions about his journey, and busied herself in setting a chair for him by the fire, putting
his hat aside, and begging him to take off his overcoat. He complied. As he threw the coat on a
chair, he said, with a very moderately successful
attempt at pleasantry:

"I have come back richer than I went, Mrs.
Routh, by that elegant garment, and no more."

"Bowled out, eh?" asked Routh, taking the cigar from his mouth, and laying it on the mantel-piece.

"Stumped, sir," replied Dallas.

Harriet said nothing.

"That's bad, Dallas."

"Very bad, my dear fellow, but very true. Look here," the young man continued, with earnestness, "I don't know what to do. I don't upon my soul! I saw my mother—"

"Yes?" said Harriet, going up to his side. "Well?"

"I saw her, and—and she is unable to help me; she is, indeed, Mrs. Routh," for a bitter smile was on Harriet's face, turned full upon him. "She hasn't the means. I never understood her position until last night, but I understood it then. She is —" he stopped. All his better nature forbad his speaking of his mother's position to these people. Her influence, the gentler, better influence, was over him still. However transitory it might prove, it had not passed yet. Harriet Routh knew as well as he did what the impulse was that arrested his speech.

"You will tell me all about it yet," she thought, and not a sign of impatience appeared in her face.

"I—I need not bore you with details," he went on. "She could not give me the money. She made me understand that. But she promised to get it for me, in some way or other, if the thing is within the reach of possibility, before a month expires. I know she will do it, but I must give her time, if it's to be forthcoming, and you must give me time."

"It's unfortunate, Dallas," Routh began, in a cold voice, "and, of course, it's all very well your talking to me about giving you time, but how am *I* to get it? It's no good going over the old story, you know it as well as I do. There, there," he said, shrugging his shoulders, "I must try and get old Shadrach to renew. I suppose we may as well go at once, Dallas." He left the room, followed by Harriet.

George Dallas sat over the fire in an attitude of deep dejection. He was sick at heart, and the revulsion of feeling that had begun at Poynings had not yet ceased. "If I could but be done with it all!" he thought. "But I'm in the groove, I'm in the groove."

"Come along, George," said Routh, who seemed more good humoured than before, as he reëntered the room, soberly attired, as became a man going to do business in the City. "Don't be down-hearted; the old lady will keep her word. Don't be afraid; and, in the mean time, we'll pull through. Put your coat on, and come along. You'll give us some dinner, Harriet, won't you? And if Deane calls, ask him to join us. He won't," he continued, with a laugh, "because he believes in tavern dinners, and puts no faith in ours. We're snobs who live in lodgings, George, you know; but he'll drop in in the evening fast enough."

The application to Mr. Shadrach proved successful, and George Dallas returned with Stewart Routh to his lodgings, more firmly tied to him than ever, by the strong bond of an increased money-obligation.

"Pretty tidy terms, weren't they?" Routh asked Dallas, when he had told Harriet, in answer to her anxious questioning, that the "renewal" had been arranged.

"Very tidy indeed," said poor George, ruefully: "but, Routh, suppose when I do get the
money, it's not enough. What's to be done
then?"

"Never mind about *then*," said Routh, "*now* is
the important matter. Remember that every *then*
is made of *nows*, and keep your mind easy. That's
philosophy, as Mr. Squeers says. Your present
business is to eat your dinner."

Stewart Routh had thrown off his low spirits,
and had all but succeeded in rousing George
Dallas from his. Kindly, convivial, only occasionally coarse, he was a dangerously pleasant man
at all times, and especially so to George Dallas
when Harriet was present; for then his coarseness
was entirely laid aside, and her tact, humour, intelligence never failed to please, to animate, and
to amuse him. The dinner was a very pleasant
one, and, before it had come to a conclusion, George
Dallas began to yield as completely as ever to the
influence of the man whose enviable knowledge
of "life" had been the first medium through
which he had attained it. George had forgotten
the renewed bill and his late failure for a while,

when the mention of Deane's name recalled it to his memory.

"Has Deane been here, Harry?" asked Routh.

"No, Stewart, I have been at home all day, but he has not called."

"Ah—didn't happen to want me, no doubt."

"Have you seen much of him lately, Routh?" inquired George Dallas. "I mean, within the last week or two? While I—while I've been keeping out of the way?" he said, with a nervous laugh.

"Poor boy, you *have* been down on your luck," said Routh. "Seen much of Deane? O, yes; he's always about—he's here most days, some time in the forenoon."

"In the forenoon, is he? Considering the hours he keeps at night, that surprises me."

"It doesn't surprise *me*. He's very strong—has a splendid constitution, confound him, and has not given it a shake yet. Drink doesn't seem to 'trouble' him in the least."

"He's an odd fellow," said George, thoughtfully. "How coolly he won my money, and what a greenhorn I was, to be sure! I wonder if he would have lost his own so coolly."

"Not a doubt of it," said Routh; "he'd have been satisfied he would make it up out of something else. He *is* an odd fellow, and a duced unpleasant fellow to *my* mind."

Harriet looked at her husband with a glance of caution. It was unlike Routh to dwell on a mere personal feeling, or to let so much of his mind be known unnecessarily. He caught the glance and understood it, but it only angered, without otherwise influencing him.

"A low-lived loafer, if ever there was one," he went on, "but useful in his way, Dallas. Every man has a weakness; *his* is to think himself a first-rate billiard player, while he is only a fourth-rate. A man under such a delusion is sure to lose his money to anyone who plays better than he does, and I may as well be that man, don't you see?"

"I see perfectly," said George; "but I wish he had been equally mistaken in his notions of his card-playing science; it would have made a serious difference to me."

"Never mind, old fellow," answered Routh; "you shall have your revenge some day. Finish your wine, and Harriet shall give us some music."

She did so. She gave them some music, such as very few can give—music which combines perfection of art with true natural feeling. This woman was a strange anomaly, full of " treasons, stratagems, and spoils," and yet with music in her soul.

Rather early, George Dallas left the pair, but they sat up late, talking earnestly. Things were going ill with Stewart Routh. Some of his choicest and most promising combinations had failed. He had once or twice experienced a not uncommon misfortune in the lot of such men as he;—he had encountered men in his own profession who were as clever as himself, and who, favoured by circumstances and opportunity, had employed their talents at his expense. The swindler had been swindled once or twice, the biter had been bitten, and his temper had not been improved in the process. He was about, as Harriet had said, to take a new flight this time, in the direction of operations on the general public, and he had formed designs on Mr. Deane, which did not, in the increased know-

ledge he had obtained of that gentleman's character, and in the present aspect of affairs, look
quite so promising as in the early stage of their
acquaintance, six weeks before. The operations
of gentlemen of the Routh fraternity are planned
and executed with a celerity which seems extraordinary to pursuers of the more legitimate
branches of industry. Routh had not passed
many hours in Mr. Deane's society (they had met
at a low place of amusement, the honours of which
Routh was doing to a young Oxonian, full of cash
and devoid of brains, whom he had in hand just
then), before he had built an elaborate scheme
upon the slender foundation of that gentleman's
boasted wealth and assumed greenness. His sub-
sequent experience had convinced him of the
reality of the first, but had shown him his mistake as to the last, and gradually his mind, usually
cool and undaunted, became haunted by an ever-
burning desire to possess himself of the money for
ever flaunted before his eyes—became haunted,
too, by an unreasonable and blind animosity to
the stranger, who combined profligacy with calculation, unscrupulous vice with well-regulated eco-

nomy, and the unbridled indulgence of his pas-
sions with complete coldness of heart and coolness
of temper. Routh had no knowledge of Deane's
real position in life, but he had a conviction that
had it been, like his own, that of a professional
swindler, he would have been a dangerous rival,
quite capable of reducing his own occupation and
his own profits very considerably. Therefore
Routh hated him.

When the conference between Routh and Harriet came to a conclusion, it left the woman visibly
troubled. When Routh had been for some time
asleep, she still sat by the table, on which her
elbows rested, her head on her hands, and the
light shining on her fair brown hair. There she
sat, until the fire died out, and the late wintry
dawn came. She was not unused to such watches;
wakefulness was habitual to her, and care had often
kept her company. But no vigil had ever tried
her so much. Her mind was at work, and suffering. When at length she rose from her chair
with an impatient shiver, dark circles were round
her blue eyes, and her pure waxen complexion
looked thick and yellow. She lighted a candle,

turned the gas out, and went for a moment to the window. The cold grey light was beginning to steal through the shutter, which she opened wide, and then looked out. She set the candle down, and leaned idly against the window. Weariness and restlessness were upon her. The street was quite empty, and the houses opposite looked inexpressibly gloomy. "One would think all the people in them were dead instead of asleep," she said, half aloud, as she pulled the blind down with a jerk, and turned away. She went slowly upstairs to her bedroom, and as she went, she murmured:

"Where will it end? How will it end? It is an awful risk!"

CHAPTER IV.

NOT one word came from Mrs. Carruthers for full six weeks. The hope which had sprung up in George Dallas's breast after the interview with his mother in the housekeeper's room had gone through the various stages common to unfulfilled desires in men of sanguine temperaments. It had been very bright at first, and when no letter came after the lapse of a week, it had begun to grow dim, and then he had endeavoured to reason with himself that the very fact of no letter coming ought to be looked upon as a good sign, as showing that "something was doing." Then the absence of any news caused his hope to flicker until the recollection of the old adage, that "no news was good news," made it temporarily bright again; then as the time for payment of the renewed bill grew nearer and nearer, so did George Dallas's prospects become gloomier and yet more gloomy, and at last the light of hope went out, and the darkness of despair reigned paramount in his bosom. What could his mother be about? She must have pretended that she had some bill of her own to pay, and that the money was immediately required; old Carruthers must have questioned her about it, and there must have been a row; she must have tried to "collar" the amount out of the housekeeping—no! the sum was too large; that was absurd! She had old friends—people who knew and loved her well, and she must have asked some of them to lend it to her, and probably been refused; old friends always refuse to lend money. She must have tried—confound it all, he did not know, he could not guess what she had tried! All he did know, to his sorrow, was, that she had not sent the money; all he knew, to his joy, was, that though he was constantly seeing Stewart Routh, that worthy had, as yet, uttered no word of discontent at its non-appearance.

Not he! In the hand which Stewart Routh was at that moment playing in the greater game of life, the card representing a hundred and forty pounds was one on which he bestowed very little attention. It might, or it might not, form part of the odd trick, either way : but it had very little influence on his strategy and finesse. There were times when a five-pound note might have turned his chance, but this was not one of them. Driven into a corner, pressed for the means of discharging paltry debts, harassed by dunning creditors, Stewart Routh would have needed and claimed the money due to him by George Dallas. Present circumstances were more favourable, and he only needed George Dallas's assistance in his schemes. For, Stewart Routh's measures for raising money were of all kinds and of all dimensions; the elephant's trunk of his genius could pick up a five-pound-note bet from a flat at *écarté*, or could move the lever of a gigantic city swindle. And he was "in for a large thing" just at this time. Men attending professionally the betting-ring at the great steeple-chase then coming off, noticed Routh's absence with wonder, and though he occasionally looked in at two or three of the second-rate sporting clubs of which he was a member, he was listless and preoccupied. If he took a hand

at cards, though from mere habit he played closely
and cautiously, yet he made no great points, and
was by no means, as usual, the dashing Paladin
round whose chair men gathered thickly, and
whose play they backed cheerily. No! The paltry gains of the dice-box and cards paled before
the glamour of the fortune to be made in companies and shares; the elephant's trunk was to
show its strength now, as well as its dexterity,
and the genius which had hitherto been confined to
"bridging" a pack of cards, or "securing" a die,
talking over a flat or winning money of a greenhorn, was to have its vent in launching a great
City Company. Of this scheme Dallas knew nothing. A disinherited man, with neither name
nor influence, would have been utterly useless;
but he was reserved for possible contingencies.
Routh was always sending to him to call, always
glad to see him when he called, and never plagued
him with allusions to his debt. But in their inter-
views nothing but mere generalities were discussed,
and George noticed that he always received a hint
to go, whenever Mr. Deane was announced.

But although Stewart Routh was seen but

seldom in his usual haunts, he was by no means
inactive or neglectful of his own interests. Day
after day he spent several hours in the City, dili-
gently engaged in the formation of his new Company, a grand undertaking for working some
newly-discovered silver mines in the Brazils; and
day after day were his careful scheming, his elaborate plotting, his vivacious daring, and his con-
summate knowledge of the world, rewarded by the
steady progress which the undertaking made. The
temporary offices in Tokenhouse-yard were be-
sieged with inquirers; good brokers with City
names of high standing offered their services;
splendid reports came from the engineers, who
had been sent out to investigate the state of the
mines. Only one thing was wanting, and that
was capital; capital, by hook or by crook, Mr.
Stewart Routh must have, and was determined
to have. If the affair were to be launched, the
brokers said, the next week must see it done;
and the difficulty of raising the funds for the
necessary preliminary expenses was becoming day
by day more and more palpable and insurmount-
able to Stewart Routh.

The interval of time that had witnessed so
much activity on the part of Mr. Stewart Routh,
and had advanced his schemes close to a condition of imminent crisis, had been productive of
nothing new or remarkable in the existence of
George Dallas.   That is to say, on the surface
of it.   He was still leading the desultory life of
a man who, with an intellectual and moral nature capable of better deeds and nobler aspirations, is incurably weak, impulsive, and swayed
by a love of pleasure; a man incapable of real
self-control, and with whom the gratification of
the present is potent, above all suggestions or con-
siderations of the contingencies of the future.   He
worked a little, and his talent was beginning to
tell on the popularity of the paper for which he
worked, The Mercury, and on the perceptions of
its proprietors.   George Dallas was a man in
whose character there were many contradictions.
With much of the fervour of the poetic temperament, with its sensuousness and its sensitiveness,
he had a certain nonchalance about him, a fitful
indifference to external things, and a spasmodic
impatience of his surroundings.   This latter was

apt to come over him at times when he was apparently merriest, and it had quite as much to
do with his anxiety to get his debt to Routh discharged, and to set himself free from Routh, as
any moral sense of the danger of keeping such
company, or any moral consciousness of the waste
of his life, and the deterioration of his character.
George Dallas had no knowledge of the true history of Routh's career; of the blacker shades of
his character he was entirely ignorant. In his
eyes, Routh was a clever man, and a good-for-
nothing, a "black sheep" like himself, a sheep
for whose blackness Dallas (as he did in his own
case) held circumstances, the white sheep, anything and everything except the man himself, to
blame. He was dimly conscious that his associate
was stronger than he, stronger in will, stronger in
knowledge of men, and somehow, though he never
defined or acknowledged the feeling. to himself,
he mistrusted and feared him. He liked him, too,
he felt grateful to him for his help; he did not
discern the interested motives which actuated him,
and, indeed, they were but small, and would by
no means have accounted for all Routh's proceed-

ings towards Dallas. Nor is it necessary that they should; a villain is not, therefore, altogether precluded from likings, or even the feebler forms of friendship, and Dallas was not simply silly and egotistical when he believed that Routh felt kindly and warmly towards him. Still, whether a merciful and occult influence was at work within him, or the tide of his feelings had been turned by his stolen interview with his mother, by his being brought into such positive contact with her life and its conditions, and having been made to realise the bitterness he had infused into it, it were vain to inquire. Whatever his motives, however mixed their nature or confused their origin, he was filled, whenever he was out of Routh's presence, and looked his life in the face, with an ardent longing to "cut the whole concern," as he phrased it in his thoughts. And Harriet?—for the "whole concern" included her, as he was forced to remember—Harriet, the only woman whose society he liked—Harriet, whom he admired with an admiration as pure and respectful as he could have felt for her, had he met her in the least equivocal, nay, even in the most exalted position. Well, he would be very sorry to lose Harriet, but, after all, she cared only for Routh; and he was dangerous. "I must turn over a new leaf, for *her* sake" (he meant for his mother's); "and I can't turn it while they are at my elbows." From which conviction on the part of George it is sufficiently evident that Routh and Harriet had ample reason to apprehend that Dallas, on whom they desired to retain a hold, for more reasons than one, was slipping through their fingers.

George Dallas was more than usually occupied with such thoughts one morning, six weeks after his unsuccessful visit to Poynings. He had been very much with Routh and Deane during this period, and yet he had begun to feel aware, with a jealous and suspicious sense of it, too, that he really knew very little of what they had been about. They met in the evening, in pursuit of pleasure, and they abandoned themselves to it; or they met at Routh's lodgings, and Dallas surrendered himself to the charm which Harriet's society always had for him. But he had begun to observe of late that there was no reference to the occupation of the earlier part of the day, and that while there was apparently a close bond of mutual confidence or convenience between Routh and Deane, there was some under-current of mutual dislike.

"If my mother can only get me out of this scrape, and I can get the *Piccadilly* people to take my serial," said George Dallas to himself one morning, when April was half gone, and "the season" was half come, "I shall get away somewhere, and go in for work in earnest." He looked, ruefully enough, round the wretched little bedroom, at whose small window he was standing, as he spoke; and he thought impatiently of his debt to his coarse shrewish landlady, and of the small liabilities which hampered him as effectually as the great one. It was later than his usual hour of rising, and he felt ill and despondent: not anxious to face the gay, rich, busy world outside, and still less inclined for his own company and waking thoughts in the shabby little den he tenanted. A small room, a mere apology for a sitting-room, was reached through a rickety folding-door, which no human ingenuity could contrive to keep shut if any one opened the other door

leading to the narrow passage, and the top of
the steep dark staircase. Through this yawning
aperture George lounged disconsolately into the
little room beyond, eyeing with strong disfavour
the preparations for his breakfast, which preparations chiefly consisted of a dirty table-cloth
and a portion of a stale loaf, popularly known
as a "heel." But his gaze travelled further, and
brightened; for on the cracked and blistered
wooden chimney-piece lay a letter in his mother's
hand. He darted at it, and opened it eagerly,
then held it for a moment in his hand unread.
His face turned very pale, and he caught his
breath once or twice as he muttered:

"Suppose it's to say she can't do anything at
all." But the fear, the suspense were over with
the first glance at his mother's letter. She wrote:

"Poynings, 13th April 1861.

"MY DEAR GEORGE,—I have succeeded in
procuring you the money, for which you tell me
you have such urgent need. Perhaps if I admired,
and felt disposed to act up to a lofty standard of
sentimental generosity, I should content myself

with making this announcement, and sending you
the sum which you assure me will release you from
your difficulties, and enable you to commence the
better life on which you have led me to hope you
are resolved.   But not only do the circumstances
under which I have contrived to get this money
for you make it impossible for me to act in this
way, but I consider I should be very wrong, and
quite wanting in my duty, if I failed to make you
understand, at the cost of whatever pain to myself,
the price I have had to pay for the power of aid-
ing you.

"You have occasioned me much suffering,
George. You, my only child, to whom I looked
in the first dark days of my early bereavement,
with such hope and pride as I cannot express, and
as only a mother can understand—you have darkened my darkness and shadowed my joy, you have
been the source of my deepest anxiety, though not
the less for that, as you well know, the object of
my fondest love. I don't write this to reproach
you—I don't believe in the efficacy of reproach;
but merely to tell you the truth—to preface another truth, the full significance of which it may

prove very beneficial to you to understand. Sorrow I have known through you, and shame I have experienced for you. You have cost me many tears, whose marks can never be effaced from my face or my heart ; you have cost me infinite disappointment, bitterness, heart-sickness, and domestic wretchedness; but now, for the first time, you cost me shame on my own account. Many and great as my faults and shortcomings have been through life, deceit was equally abhorrent to my nature and foreign to my habits. But for you, George, for your sake, to help you in this strait, to enable you to release yourself from the trammels in which you are held, I have descended to an act of deceit and meanness, the recollection of which must for ever haunt me with a keen sense of humiliation. I retain enough of my former belief in you, my son, to hope that what no other argument has been able to effect, this confession on my part may accomplish, and that you, recognising the price at which I have so far rescued you, may pause, and turn from, the path leading downward into an abyss of ruin, from which no effort of mine could avail to snatch you. I have procured the money you re-

quire, by an expedient suggested to me accident-
ally, just when I had begun utterly to despair of
ever being able to accomplish my ardent desire,
by a conversation which took place at dinner between Mr. Carruthers and his family solicitor, Mr.
Tatham. The conversation turned on a curious
and disgraceful family story which had come under
his knowledge lately. I need not trouble you to
read, nor myself to write, its details; you will
learn them when I see you, and give you the
money; and I do not doubt, I dare not doubt,
George, that you will feel all I expect you to feel
when you learn to how deliberate, laborious, and
mean a deception I have descended for your sake.
I can never do the same thing again; the expedient is one that it is only possible to use once, and
which is highly dangerous even in that one instance. So, if even you were bad and callous
enough to calculate upon a repetition of it, which I
could not believe, my own dear boy, I am bound
to tell you that it never could be. Unless Mr.
Carruthers should change his mind, consequent
upon an entire, radical, and most happy change in
your conduct, all pecuniary assistance on my part

must be entirely impossible. I say this, thus strongly, out of the kindest and best motives towards you. Your unexpected appearance and application agitated and distressed me very much; not but that the sight of you, under any circumstances, must always give me pleasure, however closely pursued and overtaken by pain. For several days I was so completely upset by the recollection of your visit, and the strong and desperate necessity that existed for repressing all traces of such feelings, that I was unable to think over the expedients by which I might procure the money you required. Then as I began to grow a little quieter, accident gave me the hint upon which I have acted secretly and safely. Come down to Poynings in three days from this time. Mr. Carruthers is at present away at an agricultural meeting at York, and I can see you at Amherst, without difficulty or danger. Go to the town, but not to the inn. Wait about until you see my carriage. This is the 13th. I shall expect you on the 17th, by which day I hope to have the money ready for you.

"And now, my dear boy, how shall I end this

letter? What shall I say? What can I say that
I have not said again and again, and with sadly
little effect, as you will not deny? But I forbear,
and I hope. A feeling that I cannot define, an
instinct, tells me that a crisis in my life is near.
And what can such a crisis in my life mean, except in reference to you, my beloved and only
child? In your hands lies all the future, all the
disposition of the 'few and evil' years which remain to me. How are you going to deal with
them? Is the love, which can never fail or falter,
to be tried and wounded to the end, George, or is
it to see any fruition in this world? Think over
this question, my son, and let me read in your
face, when I see you, that the answer is to be one
of hope. You are much changed, George, the
bitterness is succeeding the honey in your mouth;
you are 'giving your strength for that which is
not meat, and your labour for that which satisfieth
not,' and though all the lookers-on at such a career
as yours can see, and always do see, its emptiness
and insufficiency plainly, what does their wisdom,
their experience, avail? But if wisdom and experience come *to yourself*, that makes all the differ-

ence. If *you* have learned, and I venture to hope
you *have*, that the delusive light is but a 'Will of
the Wisp,' you will cease to pursue it. Come to
me, then, my boy. I have kept my word to you,
at such a cost as you can hardly estimate, seeing
that no heart can impart *all* its bitterness to another; will you keep yours to me?

"C. L. CARRUTHERS."

"What does she mean? What can she mean?"
George Dallas asked himself this question again
and again, as he stood looking at the letter in his
hand. "What *has* she done? A mean and deliberate deceit — some dishonourable transaction?
My mother could not do anything deserving to be
so called. It is impossible. Even if she could
contemplate such a thing, she would not know how
to set about it. God bless her!"

He sat down by the table, drew the dingy
Britannia-metal teapot over beside his cup, and sat
with his hand resting idly upon the distorted
handle, still thinking less of the relief which the
letter had brought him, than of the mysterious
terms in which it was couched.

" She can't have got it out of Carruthers without his knowing anything about it ?" he mused.
" No ; besides, getting it from *him* at all, is precisely the thing she told me she could not do.
Well, I must wait to know; but how good of her
to get it ! Who's the fellow who says a man can
have only one mother ? By Jove, how right he is !"

Then George ate his breakfast hastily, and,
putting the precious letter in his breast-pocket,
went to Routh's lodgings.

" I dare say they're not up," he thought, as he
knocked at the door, and patiently awaited the
lingering approach of the slipshod servant. " Routh
was as late as I was last night, and I know she
always sits up for him."

He was right; they had not yet appeared in
the sitting-room, and he had time for a good deal
of walking up and down, and much cogitation over
his mother's letter, before Harriet appeared. She
was looking anxious, Dallas thought, so he stepped
forward even more eagerly than usual, and told
her in hurried tones of gladness that the post had
brought him good news, and that his mother was
going to give him the money.

"I don't know how she has contrived to get it, Mrs. Routh," he said.

"Does she not tell you, then?" asked Harriet, as she eyed with some curiosity the letter which Dallas had taken out of his pocket, and which he turned about in his hand, as he stood talking to her. As she spoke, he replaced the letter in his pocket, and sat down.

"No," he answered, moodily, "she does not; but she did not get it easily, I know—not without a very painful self-sacrifice; but here's Routh."

"Ha! Dallas, my boy," said Routh, after he had directed one fleeting glance of inquiry towards his wife, and almost before he had fairly entered the room. "You're early—any news?"

"Very good news," replied Dallas; and he repeated the information he had already given Harriet. Routh received it with a somewhat feigned warmth, but Dallas was too much excited by his own feelings to perceive the impression which the news really produced on Routh.

"Is your letter from the great Mr. Carruthers himself?" said Routh; "from the provincial magnate who has the honour of being step-father to you—your magnificent three-tailed bashaw?"

"O dear no!" said the young man grimly; "not from him. My letter is from my mother."

"And what has she to say?" asked Harriet quickly.

"She tells me she will very shortly be able to let me have the sum I require."

"The deuce she will!" said Routh. "Well, I congratulate you, my boy! I may say I congratulate all of us, for the matter of that; but it's rather unexpected, isn't it? I thought Mrs. Carruthers told you, when you saw her so lately, that the chances of her bleeding that charming person, her husband, were very remote."

"She did say so, and she was right; it's not from him she's going to get the money. Thank Heaven for that!"

"Certainly, if you wish it, though I'm not sure that we're right in being over-particular whence the money comes, so that it does come when one wants it. What is that example in the Eton Latin Grammar—'I came to her in season, which is the chief thing of all?' But if not from Mr. Carruthers, where does she get the money?"

"I—I don't know; but she does not get it without some horrible self-sacrifice; you may depend on that."

"My dear George, Mrs. Carruthers's case is not a singular one. We none of us get money without an extraordinary amount of self-sacrifice."

"Not a singular one! No, by George, you're right there, Routh," said the young man bitterly; "but does that make it any lighter for her to bear, or any better for me to reflect upon? There are hundreds of vagabond sons in England at this moment, I dare say, outcasts—sources of shame and degradation to their mothers, utterly useless to any one. I swear, when I think of what my mother must have gone through to raise this money, when I think of the purpose for which it is required, I thoroughly loathe myself, and feel inclined to put a pistol to my head, or a razor to my throat. However, once free, I—there—that's the old cant again!"

As the young man said these words, he rose from his chair, and fell to pacing the room with

long strides. Stewart Routh tooked up sternly at
him from under his bent brows, and was about to
speak; but Harriet held up a finger deprecatingly,
and when George Dallas seated himself again,
and, with his face on his hands, remained moodily
gazing at the table, she stole behind him and laid
her hand on his shoulder.

"I know you would not intentionally wound
me, Mr. Dallas," she said. "I say, you would not
intentionally wound *me*," she repeated, apparently
in answer to his turning sharply round and staring
at her in surprise; "but you seem to forget that
it was I who counselled your recent visit to your
mother, and suggested your asking her for this
sum of money, which you were bound in honour
to pay, and without the payment of which you—
who have always represented yourself as most dear
to her—would have been compromised for ever.
I am sorry I did so, now that I see my intentions
were misunderstood, and I say so frankly."

"I swear to you, Har—Mrs. Routh—I had
not the slightest idea of casting the least imputa-
tion on your motives; I was only thinking——
You know I'm a little hot on the subject of my

mother, not without reason, perhaps, for she's been a perfect angel to me, and—one can't expect other people to enter into these things, and, of course, it was very absurd. But you must forget it, please, Mrs. Routh, and you too, Stewart. If I spoke sharply or peevishly, don't mind it, old fellow!"

"I?" said Routh, with a crisp laugh. "I *don't* mind it; and I dare say I was very provoking; but you see I never knew what it was to have a mother, and I'm not much indebted to my other parent. As to the money, George—these are hard times, but if the payment of it is to drive a worthy lady to distress, or is to promote discord between you and me, why, in friendship's name, keep it, I say!"

"You're a good fellow, Stewart," said Dallas, putting out his hand; "and you, Mrs. Routh, have forgiven me?" Though she only bowed her head slightly, she looked down into his face with a long, steady, earnest gaze. "There's an end of it, then, I trust," he continued; "we never have had words here, and I hope we're not going to begin now. As for the money, that must be. paid. Whatever my mother has had to do is as good as done, and need not be whined over. Besides, I know you want the money, Stewart."

"That's simply to say that I am in my normal state. I always want money, my dear George."

"You shall have this, at all events. And now I must be off, as I have some work to do for the paper. See you very soon again. Good-bye, Stewart. The cloud has quite passed away, Mrs. Routh?"

She said "Quite," as she gave him her hand, and their eyes met. There was eager inquiry in his glance; there was calm, steadfast earnestness in hers. Then he shook hands with Routh, and left the room.

The moment the door closed behind him, the smile faded away from Routh's face, and the stern look which it always wore when he was preoccupied and thoughtful settled down upon it. For a few minutes he was silent; then he said in a low voice: "Harriet, for the first time in your life, I suppose, you very nearly mismanaged a bit of business I intrusted to you."

His wife looked at him with wonder-lifted

brows. "I, Stewart? Not intentionally, I need not tell you. But how?"

"I mean this business of George's. Did not you advise him to go down and see his mother?"

"I did. I told him he must get the money from her."

"A mistake, Harry, a mistake!" said Routh, petulantly. "Getting the money means paying us; paying us, means breaking with us?"

"Breaking with us?"

"Nothing less. Did you not hear him when the remorseful fit was on him just now? And don't you know that he's wonderfully young, considering all things, and has kept the bloom on his feelings in a very extraordinary manner? Did you not hear him mutter something about 'once free'? I did not like that, Harry."

"Yes, I heard him say those words," replied Harriet. "It was my hearing them that made me go up to him and speak as I did."

"That was quite right, and had its effect. One does not know what he might have done if he had turned rusty just then. And it is essential that there should not be a rupture between us now."

"George Dallas shall not dream of breaking with us; at least, he shall not carry out any such idea; I will take care of that," said Harriet, "though I think you overrate his usefulness to us."

"Do I? I flatter myself there is no man in London forced to gain his bread by his wits who has a better eye for a tool than myself. And I tell you, Harry, that during all the time we have been leading this shifty life together, we have never had any one so suitable to our purposes as George Dallas."

"He is certainly wonderfully amenable."

"Amenable? He is a good deal more than that; he is devoted. You know whose doing that is, Harry, and so do I. Why, when you laid your hand on his shoulder I saw him shiver like a leaf, and the first few words from you stilled what I thought was going to be a heavy storm."

She looked up anxiously into his face, but the smile had returned to his lips, and his brow was unclouded. Not perfectly satisfied, she suffered her eyes to drop again.

"I know perfectly well," pursued Routh, "that

the manner in which Dallas has stuck to us has been owing entirely to the influence you have over him, and which is natural enough. He is a bright young fellow, impressionable as we all are——" again her eyes were raised to his face, "—at his age; and though from the scrapes he has got into, and his own natural love of play (more developed in him than in any other man I ever met), though these things keep him down, he is innately a gentleman. You are the only woman of refinement and education to whose society he has access, and as, at the same time, you have a sweet face and an enormous power of will, it is not extraordinary that he should be completely under your influence."

"Don't you overrate that same influence, Stewart?" she asked with a faint smile.

"No man knows better how to appraise the value of his own goods—and you are my goods, are you not, Harry, and out and away, the best of all my goods? Not that that's saying much. No; I understand these things, and I understand you, and having perfect confidence and trust in you, I stand by and watch the game."

"And you're never jealous, Stewart?" she asked, with a half laugh, but with the old expression of anxious interest in her eyes.

"Jealous, Harry? Not I, my love! I tell you, I have perfect trust and confidence in you, and I know your thorough devotion to our affairs. Let us get back to what we were talking about at first—what was it exactly?"

Her eyes had dropped again at the commencement of his reply, but she raised them as he finished speaking, and said, "We were discussing the amount of George Dallas's usefulness to us."

"Exactly. His usefulness is greater than it seems. There is nothing so useful in a life like ours as the outward semblance of position. I don't mean the mere get up; that, most fools can manage; but the certain something which proclaims to his fellows and his inferiors that a man has had education and been decently bred. There are very few among our precious acquaintances who could not win Dallas's coat off his back, at cards, or billiards, or betting, but there is not one whom I could present to any young fellow of the smallest appreciation whom I might pick up. Even if their frightful appearance were not sufficiently against them—and it is—they would say or do something in the first few minutes which would awake suspicion, whereas Dallas, even in his poverty-stricken clothes of the last few weeks, looks like a gentleman, and talks and behaves like one."

" Yes," said Harriet, reflecting, " he certainly does; and that's a great consideration, Stewart?"

" Incalculable! Besides, though he is a thorough gambler at heart, he has some other visible profession. His ' connection with the press,' as he calls it, seems really to be a fact; he could earn a decent salary if he stuck to it. From a letter he showed me, I make out that they seem to think well of him at the newspaper office; and mind you, Harriet, he might be uncommonly useful to us some day in getting things kept out of the papers, or flying a few rumours which would take effect in the money-market or at Tattersall's. Do you see all that, Harry?"

" I see it," she replied; " I suppose you're right."

" Right? Of course I am! George Dallas is

the best ally—and the cheapest—we have ever
had, and he must be kept with us."

"You harp upon that 'kept with us.' Are
you still so persuaded that he wishes to shake us
off?"

"I am. I feel convinced, from that little out-
burst to-night, that he is touched by this unexplained sacrifice on the part of his mother, and
that in his present frame of mind he would give
anything to send us adrift and get back into decent life. I feel this so strongly, Harriet," continued Routh, rising from his seat, crossing to the
mantleshelf, and taking a cigar, "that I think
even your influence would be powerless to restrain
him, unless——"

"Unless what? Why do you pause?" she
asked, looking up at him with a clear steadfast
gaze.

"Unless," said Routh, slowly puffing at his
newly-lighted cigar, "unless we get a fresh and a
firm hold on him. He will pay that hundred and
forty pounds. Once paid, that hold is gone, and
with it goes our ally!"

"I see what you mean," said Harriet, after a

pause, with a short mirthless laugh. "He must be what they call in the East 'compromised.' We are plague-stricken. George Dallas must be seen to brush shoulders with us. His garments must be known to have touched ours. Then the uninfected will cast him out, and he will be reduced to herd with us."

"You are a figurative, Harry, but forcible: you have hit my meaning exactly. But the main point still remains — *how* is he to be 'compromised'?"

"It is impossible to settle that hurriedly," she replied, pushing her hair back from her forehead. "But it must be done effectually, and the step which he is led to take, and which is to bind him firmly to us, must be irrevocable. Hush! Come in!"

These last words were in reply to a knock at the room door. A dirty servant-girl put her tangled head into the room, and announced "Mr. Deane" as waiting down-stairs. This statement was apparently incorrect, for the girl had scarcely made it before she disappeared, as though pulled back, and a man stepped past her, and made one

stride into the middle of the room, where he stood
looking round him with a suspicious leer.

He was a young man, apparently not more
than two or three-and-twenty, judging by his
figure and his light active movements; but cun-
ning and deceit had stamped such wrinkles round
his eyes, and graven such lines round his mouth,
as are seldom to be seen in youth. His eyes, of a
greenish-gray hue, were small and deeply sunk in
his head; his cheek-bones were high, his cheeks
fringed by a very small scrap of whisker running
into a dirt-coloured tuft of hair growing underneath his chin. His figure was tall and angular,
his arms and legs long and awkward, his hands
and feet large and ill-shaped. He wore a large
thick overcoat with broad fur collar and cuffs,
and a hood (also fur-lined) hanging back on his
shoulders. With the exception of a very slight
strip of ribbon, he had no cravat underneath his
long limp turnover collar, but stuck into his shirt-
front was a large and handsome diamond pin.

"Why, what the 'tarnal," he commenced, placing his arms a-kimbo and without removing his
hat—"what the 'tarnal, as they say down west, is

the meaning of this little game? I come here pretty smart often, don't I? I come in gen'lly right way, don't I? Why does that gal go totin' up in front of me to-day to see if you would see me, now?"

"Some mistake, eh?"

"Not a bit of it! Gal was all right, gal was. What I want to know is, what was up? Was you you a practisin' any of your little hankey-pankeys with the pasteboards? Was you a bitin' in a double set of scrip of the new company to do your own riggin' of the market? Or was it a little bit of quiet con-nubiality with the mar-darm here in which you didn't want to be disturbed?"

Stewart Routh's face had been growing darker and darker as this speech proceeded, and at the allusion to his wife his lips began to move; but they were stopped by a warning pressure underneath the table from Harriet's foot.

"You're a queer fellow, Deane!" he said, in a subdued voice. "The fact is, we have a new servant here, and she did not recognise you as *l'ami de la maison*, and so stood on the proprieties, I suppose."

"O, that's it, eh? I don't know about the

proprieties; but when the gal knows more of me, she'll guess I'm one of 'em. Nothing improper about me—no loafin' rowdy ways such as some of your friends have. Pay my way as I go, ask no favours, and don't expect none." He gave his trousers pockets a ringing slap as he spoke, and looked round with a sneering laugh.

"There, there! It's all right; now sit down, and have a glass of wine, and tell us the news."

"No," he said, "thank'ee. I've been liquoring up in the City, where I've been doin' a little business—realising some of them Lake Eries and Michigans as I told you on. Spanking investments they were, and have turned up trumps."

"I hope you're in the hands of an honest broker," said Routh. I could introduce you to one who—"

"Thank'ee, I have a great man to broke for me, recommended to me from t'other side by his cousin who leads Wall-street, New York City. I have given him the writings, and am going to see him on Tuesday, at two, when I shall trouser the dollars to the tune of fifteen thousand and odd, if markets hold up, I reckon."

"And you'll bring some of that to us in Token-house-yard," said Routh eagerly. "You recollect what I showed you, that I—"

"O yes!" said Deane, again with the sinister smile. "You could talk a 'coon's hind leg off, you could, Routh. But I shall just keep my dollars in my desk for a few days. Tokenhouse-yeard can wait a little, can't it? just to see how things eventuate, you know."

"As you please," said Routh. "One thing is certain, Deane ; you need no Mentor in your business, whatever you may do in your pleasures."

"Flatter myself, need none in neither," said the young man, with a baleful grin. "Eh, look here, now: talking of pleasures, come and dine with me on Tuesday at Barton's, at five. I've asked Dallas, and we'll have a night of it. Tuesday, the 17th, mind. Sorry to take your husband away, Mrs. R., but I'll make up for it, some day. Perhaps you'll come and dine with me some day, Mrs. R., without R.?"

"Not I, Mr. Deane," said Harriet, with a laugh. "You're by far too dangerous a man."

Mr. Deane was gone; and again Stewart Routh sat over the table, scribbling figures on his blotting-pad.

"What are you doing, Stewart?"

"Five dollars to the pound—fifteen thousand," he said, "three thousand pounds! When did he say he would draw it?"

"On Tuesday, the—the day you dine with him."

"The day I dine with him! Keep it in his desk, he said, for a few days! He has grown very shy about Tokenhouse-yard. He hasn't been there for a week. The day I dine with him!" He had dropped his pen, and was slowly passing his hand over his chin.

"Stewart," said Harriet, going behind him and putting her arm round his neck—"Stewart, I know what thought you're busy with, but—"

"Do you, Harry?" said he, disengaging himself, but not unkindly—"do you? Then keep it to yourself, my girl, and get to bed. We must have that, Harry, in one way or another; we must have it."

She took up a candle, pressed her lips to his

forehead, and went to her room without a word. But for full ten minutes she remained standing before the dressing-table buried in thought, and again she muttered to herself: "A great risk! A great risk!"

CHAPTER V.

ON the evening of the day appointed for the dinner, Mr. Philip Deane stood on the steps of Barton's restaurant in the Strand, in anything but a contented frame of mind. His face, never too frank or genial in its expression, was puckered and set in rigid lines; his right hand was perpetually diving into his waistcoat-pocket for his watch, to which he constantly referred; while with a slight stick which he carried in his left, he kept striking his leg in an irritable and irritating manner.

Mr. Deane had cause for annoyance; it was a quarter past seven, and neither of the guests whom he had invited had as yet appeared, though the dinner had been appointed for seven sharp. Crowds of men were pouring into and out of the restaurant, the first hungry and expectant, the last placid and replete; and Mr. Deane envied the first for what they were about to receive, and the last for what they had received. Moreover, the intended diners had in several cases pushed against him with scant ceremony, and Mr. Deane was not accustomed to be pushed against; while the people who had dined eyed him, as they stood on the steps lighting their cigars, with something like compassion, and Mr. Deane was unused to be pitied. So he stood there fretting and fuming, and biting his lips and flicking his legs, until his shoulder was grasped by George Dallas, who, with as much breath as he could command—not much, for he had been running—said:

"My dear Deane! a thousand apologies for being so late! Not my own fault, I protest!"

"Never is, of course," said Mr. Deane.

"Really it was not in this instance. I went round to the *Mercury* office to look at some proofs, and they kept me to do an article on a subject which I had had the handling of before, and which—"

"No one else could handle arter you, eh? Pretty tall opinion you newspaper-writin' fellows

have of yourselves! And why didn't you bring
Routh with you when you did come?"

"Routh? I haven't seen him for three days.
Isn't he here?"

"Not he! I've been coolin' myself on this
a'mighty old door-step since seven o'clock, only
once goin' inside just to look round the saloon,
and I've not set eyes on him yet."

"How very odd!"

"So very odd, that I'll see him somethingest
before I wait for him any longer! Come you in
with me. I took a table right slick opposite the
door, and we'll go and strike up at once."

He turned on his heel as he spoke, and walked
up the passage into the large coffee-room of the
restaurant. Dallas, who followed him closely, noticed him pause for an instant before one of the
looking-glasses in the passage, put his hat a little
more on one side, and throw open the folds of his
fur-lined coat. Beneath this noticeable garment
Mr. Deane wore a large baggy suit of black, an
open-worked shirt-front with three large diamond
studs in it, a heavy gold watch-chain. There was
a large diamond ring on the little finger of each

hand. Thus tastefully attired, Mr. Deane, swaggering easily up the centre of the coffee-room and slapping his leg with his stick as he went, at length stopped at a vacant table, and clinked a knife against a tumbler.

"Now, waiter! Just look smart and slippy, and bring up our dinner right away. One of my friends is here, and I'm not a-goin' to wait for the other. He must take his chance, he must; but bring up ours at once, d'ye hear? Why, what on airth is *this*?"

"This" was a boy of about twelve years of age, with a dirty face and grimy hands, with an old peakless cap on its head, and a very shiny, greasy, ragged suit on its back. "This" seemed to have been running hard, and was out of breath, and was very hot and damp in the face. Following Mr. Deane's glance, the waiter's eyes lighted on "this," and that functionary immediately fell into wrathful vernacular.

"Hullo! what are you doing here?" said he. "Come, you get out of this, d'ye hear?"

"I hear," said the boy, without moving a muscle. "Don't you flurry yourself in that way often, or you'll bust! And what a go that'd be! You should think of your precious family, you should!"

"Will you—"

"No, I won't, and that's all about it. Here, guv'nor"—to Deane—"you're my pitch; I've brought this for you." As he said this, the boy produced from his pocket a bit of string, a pair of musical bones, and a crumpled note, and handed the latter to Deane, who stepped aside to the nearest gas-jet to read it. To the great indignation of the waiter, the boy sat himself down on the edge of a chair, and, kicking his legs to and fro, surveyed the assembled company with calm deliberation. He appeared to be taking stock generally of everything round him. Between his dirty finger and thumb he took up a corner of the tablecloth, then he passed his hand lightly over Dallas's overcoat, which was lying on an adjacent chair. This gave the waiter his chance of bursting out again.

"Leave that coat alone, can't you? Can't you keep your fingers off things that don't belong to you? Thought it was your own, perhaps, didn't you?" This last remark, in a highly sarcastic tone, as he lifted the coat from the chair and was about to carry it to a row of pegs by the door. "This ain't your mark, I believe? Your tailor don't live at Hamherst, does he?"

"Never mind my tailor, old cock! P'raps you'd like my card, but I've 'appened to come out without one. But you can have my name and address—they're wery haristocratic, not such as you're used to. Jim Swain's my name—Strike-alight Jim—60 Fullwood's-rents. Now, tell me who's your barber!" The waiter, who had a head as bald as a billiard-ball, was highly incensed at this remark (which sent some young men at an adjoining table into roars of laughter), and he would probably have found some means of venting his wrath, had not a sharp exclamation from Deane called off his attention.

"Get up dinner, waiter, at once, and clear off this third place, d'ye hear? The other gentleman ain't comin'. Now, boy, what are you waiting for?"

"No answer to go back, is there, guv'nor?"

"Answer? No; none."

"All right. Shall I take that sixpence of you now, or will you give it me to-morrow? Short reck'nings is my motter. So if you're goin' to give it, hand it over."

Unable to resist a smile, Deane took a small coin from his purse and handed it to the boy, who looked at it, put it in his pocket, nodded carelessly to Deane and Dallas, and departed, whistling loudly.

"Routh is not coming, I suppose?" said Dallas as they seated themselves at the table.

"No, he has defected, like a cussed skunk as he is, after giving me the trouble to order his dinner, which I shall have to pay for all the same. Regular riles me that does, to be put in the hole for such a one-horse concern as Mr. Routh. He ought to know better than to play such tricks with me."

"Perhaps he is compelled to absent himself. I know—"

"Compelled! That might do with some people, but it won't nohow do with me. I allow no man to put a rudeness on me. Mr. Routh wants more of me than I do of him, as I'll show him before long. He wants me to come to his rooms to-morrow night—that's for his pleasure and profit, I guess, not mine—just depends on the humour I'm in. Now here's the dinner. Let's get at it at once. There's been no screwin' nor scrapin' in the ordering of it, and you can just give Routh a back-hander next time you see him by telling him how much you liked it."

Deane unfolded his table napkin with a flourish, and cleared a space in front of him for his plate. There was an evil expression on his face; a mordant, bitter, savage expression, which Dallas did not fail to remark. However, he took no notice of it, and the conversation during dinner was confined to ordinary commonplaces.

Mr. Deane had not boasted without reason; the dinner was excellent, the wines were choice and abundant, and with another kind of companion George Dallas would have enjoyed himself. But even in the discussion of the most ordinary topics there was a low coarseness in Deane's conversation, a vulgar self-sufficiency and delight at his own shrewdness, a miserable mistrust of every one, and a general arrogance and conceit which were highly nettling and repulsive. During dinner these amiable qualities displayed themselves in Mr. Deane's communication with the waiter; it was not until the cloth had been removed, and they were taking their first glass of port, that Deane reverted to what had annoyed him before they sat down.

"That Routh's what they call a mean cuss, t'other side the water," he commenced; "a mean cuss he is, and nothing else. Throwing me over in this way at the last minute, and never sending word before, so that I might have said we shall only be two instead of three, and saved paying for him! He thinks he's cruel wide awake, he does; but though he's been at it all his life, and it's not six months since I first caught sight of this little village nominated London, I don't think there's much he could put me up to now!"

He looked so expectant of a compliment, that Dallas felt bound to say: "You certainly seem to have made the most of your time!"

"Made the most of my time! I reckon I have! Why, there's no s'loon, oyster-cellar, dancing-shop, night-house of any name at all, where I'm not regular well known. 'Here's the Yankee,' they say, when I come in; not that I'm that, but I've told 'em I hail from the U-nited States, and that's why they call me the Yankee. They know me, and they know I pay my way as I go, and that I've got plenty of money. Help yourself—good port this, ain't it?—ought to be, for they charge eight shillings a bottle for it. Why people out t'other side the water, sir, they think I'm staying in titled country-houses, and dining in Portland-place, and going to hear oratorios. I've got letters of introduction in my desk which would do all that, and more. Never mind! I like to shake a loose leg, and, as I flatter myself I can pretty well take care of myself, I shake it!"

"Yes," said Dallas, in a slightly bitter tone, with a vivid recollection of his losses at cards to Deane; "yes, you can take care of yourself."

"Rather think so," repeated Deane, with a jarring laugh. "There are two things which are guiding principles with me—number one, never to lend a dollar to any man; number two, always to have the full value of every dollar I spend. If you do that, you'll generally find yourself not a loser in the end. We'll have another bottle of this eight-shilling port. I've had the value of this dinner out of you, recollect, so that I'm not straying from my principle. Here, waiter, another bottle of this eight-shilling wine!"

"You're a lucky fellow, Deane," said George Dallas, slowly finishing his second glass of the fresh bottle; "you're a lucky fellow, to have plenty of money and to be your own master, able to choose your own company, and do as you like. I wish I had the chance!" As Dallas spoke, he filled his glass again.

"Well, there are worse berths than mine in the ship, and that's a fact!" said Deane calmly. "I've often thought about you, Dallas, I have now, and I've often wondered when you'll be like the prodigal son, and go home to your father, and succeed the old man in the business."

"I have no father!"

"Hain't you though? But you've got some friends, I reckon, who are not over-delighted at

your campin' out with the wild Injuns you're living among at present?"

"I have a mother."

"That's a step towards respectability. I suppose you'll go back to the old lady, some day, and
be welcomed with open arms?"

"There's some one else to have a say in that
matter. My mother is—is married again. I have
a step-father."

"Not generally a pleasant relation, but no
reason why you shouldn't help yourself to this
eight-shilling wine. That's right; pass the bottle.
A step-father, eh? And he and you have collided
more than once, I expect?"

"Have what?"

"Collided."

"Do you mean come into collision?"

"Expect I do," said Deane calmly.

"I'm forbidden the house. I'm looked upon
as a black sheep—a pest—a contamination."

"But the old gentleman wouldn't catch anything from you. They don't take contamination
easy, after fifty!"

"O, it's not for himself that Mr. Carruthers

is anxious; he is infection proof—he——What is the matter?"

"Matter? Nothing! What name did you say?"

"Carruthers—Capel Carruthers. County family down in Kent."

"Go ahead!" said Deane, tossing off his wine, refilling his glass, and pushing the bottle to his companion; "and this old gentleman is not anxious about himself, you say; where is your bad influence likely to fall, then?"

"On his niece, who lives with them."

"What's her name?"

"Clare. Clare Carruthers! Isn't it a pretty name?"

"It is so, sir! And this niece. What's she like, now?"

George Dallas tried to throw a knowing gleam into his eyes, which the perpetual motion of the decanter had rendered somewhat bleared and vacant, as he looked across at his companion, and said with a half laugh: "You seem to take a great interest in my family, Deane?"

Not one whit discomposed, Philip Deane replied: "Study of character as a citizen of the world, and a general desire to hear what all gals are like. Is Miss Clare pretty?"

"I've only seen her once, and that not too clearly. But she struck me as being lovely."

"Lovely, eh? And the old man won't have you at any price? That's awkward, that is!"

"Awkward!" said Dallas, in a thick voice, "it's more than awkward, as he shall find! I'll be even with him—I'll——Hallo! What do you want, intruding on gentlemen's conversation?"

"Beg pardon, sir," said the waiter, to whom this last remark was addressed; "no offence, gentlemen, but going to shut up now! We ain't a supper-'ouse, gentlemen, and it's going on for twelve o'clock."

Indeed, all the other tables were vacated, so Deane rose at once and paid the bill which the waiter had laid before him. Dallas rose too with a staggering step.

"Coat, sir," said the waiter, handing it to him; "other arm, sir, please; gently does it, sir; that's it!" And with some little difficulty he pulled the coat on: George Dallas cursing it, and the country

tailor who had made it, as he stood rocking uneasily on his heels and glaring vacantly before
him.

"Come along, old horse," said Deane; "you'll
be fixed as firm as Washington Capitol when we
get into the air. Come along, and we'll go and
finish the night somewhere!"

So saying, he tucked his companion's arm
firmly within his own, and they sallied forth.

CHAPTER VI.

GEORGE DALLAS felt that his fortunes were in the
ascendant, when he arose on the morning following the dinner with Deane, and found himself
possessed of ten pounds, which he had been sufficiently sober to win at billiards the previous night,
and consequently in a position to pay off his landlady, and turn his back upon the wretched lodg-
ing, which her temper, tyranny, and meanness,
had made more wretched. He lost no time in
packing up the few articles he possessed—mainly
consisting of books and drawing-materials—and
these, together with his scanty wardrobe, he threw
into a couple of trunks, which he himself carried
down the steep dark staircase and deposited in a
cab. The landlady stood at the door, in the gray
morning, and watched her late lodger, as he strode
down the shabby little street, followed by the

luggage-laden cab. She watched him, wondering. She wondered where he had got the money he had just paid her. She wondered where he had got the money to pay an extra week's rent, in default of a week's notice. When she had dunned him yesterday, as rudely and mercilessly as usual, he had said nothing indicative of an expectation of an immediate supply of money. He had only said that he hoped to pay her soon. " Where did he get the money?" the old woman thought, as she watched him. " I hope he come by it honest. I wonder where he's going to. He did not tell the cabman, leastways so as I could hear him. Ah! It ain't no business of mine; I'll just turn the rooms out a bit, and put up the bill."

So Mrs. Gunther (for that was the lady's name) re-entered the shabby house, and a great activity accompanied by perpetual scolding pervaded it for some hours, during which the late tenant was journeying down to Amherst.

George Dallas strictly observed the directions contained in his mother's letter, and having started by an early train, reached Amherst at noon. Rightly supposing that at such an hour it would be useless to look for his mother in the little town, he crossed the railroad in a direction leading away from Amherst, struck into some fields, and wandered on by a rough footpath which led through a copse of beech-trees to a round bare hill. He sat down when he had reached this spot, from whence he could see the road to and from Poynings. A turnpike was at a little distance, and he saw a carriage stopped beside the gate, and a footman at the door receiving an order from a lady, whose bonnet he could just discern in the distance. He stood up and waited. The carriage approached, and he saw that the liveries were those of Mr. Carruthers. Then he struck away down the side of the little declivity, and crossing the railway at another point, attained the main street of the little town. It was market-day. He avoided the inn, and took up a position whence he could watch his mother's approach. There were so many strangers and what Mr. Deane would have called "loafers" about, some buying, some selling, and many honestly and unfeignedly doing nothing, that an idler more or less was certain to pass without any comment, and it was not even neces-

sary to keep very wide of the inn. He stood with
his hands in his pockets, looking into the window
of the one shop in Amherst devoted to the interests of literature, which was profusely decorated
with out-of-date valentines, much criticised by
flies, and with feebly embossed cards, setting forth
the merits of local governesses. At that time
prophetic representations of the International Exhibition of '62 were beginning to appeal to the
patriotic soul in light blue drawings, with flags
innumerable displayed wheresoever they could be
put " handy." George Dallas calmly and gravely
surveyed the stock-in-trade, rather distracted by
the process of watching the inn door, between
which and his position intervened a group of
farmers, who were to a man chewing bits of whipcord, and examining samples of corn, which they
extracted in a stealthy manner from their breeches-
pocket, and displayed grudgingly on their broad
palms. On the steps of the inn door were one or
two busy groups, and not a man or woman of the
number took any notice of Mrs. Carruthers's
son. They took very considerable notice of Mrs.
Carruthers herself, however, when her carriage

stopped; and Mr. Page, the landlord, actually came out, quite in the old-fashioned style, to open the lady's carriage, and escort her into the house. George watched his mother's tall and elegant figure, as long as she was in sight, with mingled feelings of pleasure, affection, something like real gratitude, and very real bitterness; then he turned, strolled past the inn where the carriage was being put up, and took his way down the main street, to the principal draper's shop. He went in, asked for some gloves, and turned over the packets set before him with slowness and in-decision. Presently his mother entered, and took the seat which the shopman, a mild person in spectacles, handed her. She, too, asked for gloves, and, as the shopman turned his back to the coun-ter, rapidly passed a slip of paper to her son. She had written on it, in pencil:

"At Davis's the dentist's, opposite, in ten minutes."

"These will do, thank you. I think you said three and sixpence?" said George to the shop-man, who, having placed a number of gloves before Mrs. Carruthers for her selection, had now leisure to attend to his less important customer.

"Yes, sir, three and sixpence, sir. One pair, sir? You'll find them very good wear, sir."

"One pair will do, thank you," said George. He looked steadily at his mother, as he passed her on his way to the door, and once more anger arose, fierce and keen, in his heart—anger, not directed against her, but against his step-father. "Curse him!" he muttered, as he crossed the street, "what right has he to treat me like a dog, and her like a slave? Nothing that I have done justifies—no, by Heaven, and nothing that I could do, would justify—such treatment."

Mr. Davis's house had the snug, cleanly, inflexible look peculiarly noticeable even amid the general snugness, cleanliness, and inflexibility of a country town, as attributes of the residences of surgeons and dentists, and gentlemen who combine both those fine arts. The clean servant who opened the door, looked perfectly cheerful and content. It is rather aggravating, when one is going to be tortured, even for one's ultimate good, to be assured in a tone almost of glee:

"No, sir, master's not in, sir; but he'll be in directly, sir. In the waiting-room, sir." George Dallas not having come to be tortured, and not wishing to see Mr. Davis, bore the announcement with good humour equal to that of the servant, and sat down very contentedly on a high, hard horsehair chair, to await events. Fortune again favoured him; the room had no other occupant; and in about five minutes he again heard the cheerful voice of the beaming girl at the door say,

"No, m'm, master's not in; but he'll be in d'rectly, m'm. In the waiting-room, m'm. There's one gentleman a-waitin', m'm, but master will attend on you first, of course, m'm."

The next moment his mother was in the room, her face shining on him, her arms round him, and the kind words of the truest friend any human being can be to another, poured into his ears.

"You are looking much better, George," she said, holding him back from her, and gazing fondly into his face. "You are looking brighter, my darling, and softer, and as if you were trying to keep your word to me."

"Pretty well, mother, and I am very thankful to you. But your letter puzzled me. What does it mean? Have you really got the money, and how did you manage to get it?"

"I have not got it, dear," she said quickly, and holding up her hand to keep him silent; "but it is only a short delay, not a disappointment. I shall have it in two or three days."

George's countenance had fallen at her first words, but the remainder of the sentence reassured him, and he listened eagerly as she continued:

"I am quite sure of getting it, George. If it does but set you free, I shall not regret the price I have paid for it."

"Tell me what it is, mother," George asked eagerly. "Stay, you must not sit so close to me."

"I'm not sure that your voice ought to be heard either, speaking so familiarly, tête-à-tête with the important Mrs. Carruthers of Poynings—a personage whose sayings and doings are things of note at Amherst," said Mrs. Carruthers with a smile, as he took a seat at a little distance, and placed one of the samples of periodical literature strewn about the table, after the fashion of dentists' and surgeons' waiting-rooms, ready to her hand, in case of interruption. Then she laid her clasped hands on the table, and leaned against them, with her clear dark eyes fixed upon her son's face, and her steady voice, still sweet and pure in its tones as in her youth, as she told him what she had done.

"Do you remember, George, that on that wretched night you spoke of my diamonds, and seemed to reproach me that I should wear jewels, while you wanted so urgently but a small portion of their price?"

"I remember, mother," returned George, frowning, "and a beast I was to hint such a thing to you, who gave me all that ever was your own! I hoped you had forgiven and forgotten it. Can it be possible that you have sold— But no; you said they were family jewels."

"I will tell you. When you had gone away that night, and I was in the ball-room, and later, when I was in my dressing-room alone, and could think of it all again, the remembrance of what you had said tormented me. The jewels you had seen me wearing were, indeed, as I had told you, not

my own; nevertheless, the remembrance of all I
had ever read about converting jewels into money
occupied my mind that night, and occupied it
after that night for days and days. One day Mr.
Tatham came to Poynings, and in the evening
being, as he always is, very entertaining, he re-
lated an extraordinary story of a client of his.
The tale, as he told it, had many particulars, but
one caught my attention. The client was a woman
of large fortune, who married for love a man much
younger than herself, a dissipated fellow who broke
her fortune, and might have broken her heart, but
for his getting killed in riding a steeple-chase.
After his timely death it was discovered, among a
variety of dishonourable transactions, that he had
stolen his wife's diamonds, with the connivance of
of her maid; had had them imitated in mock stones
by a famous French dealer in false jewelry; and
had substituted the false for the real. No suspicion of the fact had ever crossed his wife's mind.
The discovery was made by the jeweller's bill for
the imitation being found among his papers. This
led to inquiry of the dealer, who gave the required
information. The moment I heard the story, I

conceived the idea of getting you the money you wanted by a similar expedient."

"O, mother!"

She lifted one hand with a gesture of caution, and continued, in a voice still lower than before: ·

"*My* jewels—at least those I have sold—were my own, George. Those I wore that night were, as I told you, family diamonds; but Mr. Carruthers gave me, when we were married, a diamond bracelet, and I understood then that it was very valuable. I shrank from such a deception. But it was for you, and I caught at it."

George Dallas sat with his hands over his face and no more interrupted her by a single word.

"By one or two questions I stimulated Mr. Carruthers's curiosity in the strange story, so that he asked Mr. Tatham several questions as to where the mock jewels were made, whether they cost much, and, in fact, procured for me all the information I required. That bracelet was the only thing I had of sufficient value for the purpose, because it is expensive to get an imitation of any ornament made of very fine stones, as my bracelet is, and richly set. If the act were still

to do, I should do it, George—for you—and still
I should feel, as I do most bitterly feel, that in
doing it I shamefully deceive my husband!"

Still George Dallas did not speak. He felt
keenly the degradation to which he had reduced
his mother; but so great and pervading was his
bitterness of feeling towards his mother's husband,
that when the wrong to *him* presented itself to
his consideration, he would not entertain it. He
turned away, rose, and paced the room. His mother sighed heavily as she went on.

"George, you know this is not the first time I
have suffered through and for you, and that this
is the first time I have ever done an act which I
dare not avow. I will say no more."

He was passing behind her chair as she spoke,
and he paused in his restless walk to kneel down
by her, clasp her in his arms, and kiss her. As he
rose from his knees, she looked at him with a face
made radiant with hope, and with a mother's love.

"This is how it was done, George," she continued. "I wrote to an old friend of mine in
Paris, a French lady, once my schoolfellow. I
told her I wanted my bracelet matched, in the

best manner of imitation jewelry, as our English fashions required two, and I could not afford to purchase another made of real diamonds. I urged the strictest secrecy, and I know she will observe it; for she loves mystery only a little less than she loves dress. She undertook the commission with alacrity, and I expected to have had both the bracelets yesterday."

"What a risk you would have run, mother, supposing an occasion for your wearing the bracelet had arisen!"

"Like Anne of Austria and the studs?" said his mother with a smile. "But there was no help for it. More deceit and falsehood must have followed the first. If the occasion had arisen, Mr. Carruthers would have questioned me, and I should have said I had sent it to be cleaned, when he would have been angry that I should have done so without consulting him."

"Tyrannical old brute!" was George's mental comment.

"All the meanness and all the falsehood was planned and ready, George; but it was needless. Mr. Carruthers was summoned to York, and is

still there. It is much for me that the parcel
should arrive during his absence. I heard from
my friend, the day before I wrote to you, that she
was about to send it immediately, and I wrote to
you at once. It is to be directed to Nurse
Brookes."

"How did you explain *that*, mother?" George
asked quickly.

"More lies, more lies," she answered sadly,
rejoicing in her heart the while to see how he
writhed under the words. "I told her what was
needful in the way of false explanation, and I made
certain of having the bracelets to-day. So I must
have done but for a second letter from my friend
Madame de Haulleville, to the effect that, having
a sudden opportunity of sending the packet to
England by a private hand, she had availed herself of it, at the loss of (at most, she writes) a day
or two."

"Confound her French parsimony!" said
George; "think of the unnecessary risk she
makes us run, when I come down here for nothing."

"It is not so much parsimony as precaution,

George. And she could know nothing of any risk."

"What is to be done, then?" he asked, in a softer tone.

"Can you not remain at Amherst?" asked his mother. "Have you anything to do which will prevent your remaining here for a day or two? If not you will be as well here as in London, for there is no danger of Mr. Carruthers seeing you."

"Suppose he did?" George burst out. "Is he the lord and master of all England, including Amherst? Perhaps the sunshine belongs to him, and the fresh air? If I keep away from Poynings, that's enough for him, surely."

Mrs. Carruthers had risen, and looked appealingly at him.

"Remember, George, your misconduct would justify Mr. Carruthers in the eyes of the world, for the course he has taken towards you; or," here she moved near to him, and laid her hand on his arm, "if you refuse to consider *that*, remember that Mr. Carruthers is my husband, and that I love him."

"I will, mother, I will," said George impetuously. "Graceless, ungrateful wretch that I am! I will never say another word against him. I will remain quietly here, as you suggest. Shall I stay at the inn? Not under my own name; under my not very well known but some day of course widely to be famous pen-name—Paul Ward. Don't forget it, mother, write it down ; stay, I'll write it for you. P-a-u-l W-a-r-d." He wrote the name slowly on a slip of paper, which Mrs. Carruthers placed between the leaves of her pocket-book.

"You must go now," she said to him ; "it is impossible you can wait here longer. We have been singularly fortunate as it is. When I write, I will tell you whether I can come to you here— in the town, I mean—or whether you shall come to me. I think you will have to come to me. Now go, my darling boy." She embraced him fondly.

"And you, mother?"

"I will remain here a little longer. I have really something to say to Mr. Davis."

He went. Black care went with him, and shame and remorse were busy at his heart. Would remorse deepen into repentance, and would repentance bear wholesome fruit of reformation? That was for the future to unravel. The present had acute stinging pain in it, which he longed to stifle, to crush out, to get away from, anyhow. He loved his mother, and her beautiful earnest face went with him along the dusty road; the unshed tears in her clear dark eyes seemed to drop in burning rain upon his heart; the pleading tones of her sorrowful voice filled all the air. How wicked and wretched, how vain, silly, and insipid, how worthless and vulgar, all his pleasures and pursuits seemed now! A new spirit arose in the wayworn, jaded man; a fresh ambition sprang up in his heart. "It's a wretched, low, mean way of getting free, but I have left myself no choice. I *must* take advantage of what she has done for me, and then I never will wrong her love and generosity again. I will do right, and not wrong; this is my resolution, and I will work it out, *so help me God!*"

He had unconsciously come to a stop at the noble old oak gates, flung hospitably open, of a wide-spreading park, through one of whose vistas a grand old mansion in the most elaborate manner

of the Elizabethan style was visible. He looked
up, and the beauty of the prospect struck him as
if it had been created by an enchanter's wand.
He looked back along the road by which he had
come, and found that he had completely lost sight
of Amherst.

He went a pace or two beyond the gate pillars.
A hale old man was employed in nailing up a
trailing branch of jessamine against the porch of
the lodge.

"Good afternoon, old gentleman. This is a
fine place, I fancy."

"Good afternoon, sir. It is a fine place.
You'll not see many finer in Amherst. Would
you like to walk through it, sir? You're quite
welcome."

"Thank you. I should like to walk through
it. I have never been down this way before.
What is the name of the place, and to whom does
it belong?"

"It is called the Sycamores, sir, and it belongs
to Sir Thomas Boldero."

CHAPTER VII.

A FINE avenue of beech-trees led from the gate through which George Dallas had passed, to the house which had attracted his admiration. These grandest and most beautiful of trees were not, however, the distinguishing feature of the place : not its chief pride. " The Sycamores" was so called in honour of a profusion of trees of that kind, said in the neighbourhood to have no rivals in all England. Be that as it might, the woodland scenery in Sir Thomas Boldero's noble park was beautiful in the highest degree, and of such beauty George Dallas was keenly and artistically appreciative. The tender loveliness of the spring was abroad throughout the land; its voices, its gladness, its perfumes, were around him everywhere, and as the young man strolled on under the shadow of the great branches, bearing their tender burden of bright, soft, green, half-unclosed buds, the weight and blackness of care seemed to be lifted off him, and his heart opened to fresh, pure, simple aspirations, long strangers to his jaded but not wholly vitiated character. He was very young, and the blessed influence of youth told upon him, its power of receiving impressions, its faculty of enjoyment, its susceptibility to external things— a blessing or a curse as it is used—its buoyancy, its hopefulness. As George Dallas turned from the broad smooth carriage-way, and went wandering over the green elastic turf of the carefully kept park, winding in and out through the boles of the grand old trees, treading now on a tender twig, again on a wild flower, now startling from her nest a brooding lark, anon stopping to listen to a burst of melody from some songster free from domestic cares, he was hardly recognisable as the man who had sat listening to Philip Deane's hard worldly talk at the Strand tavern the day before.

"Brighter and softer" his mother had said he was looking, and it was true. Brighter and softer still the hard, pleasure-wearied, joyless face became, as the minutes stole over him, among the sycamores and beeches. He had pursued his desultory path a mile or more, and had lost sight of the house and the avenue, when he came to a beautiful open glade, carpeted with turf of the softest green, and over-arched by forest trees. Looking down its long vista, he saw that it terminated with a brilliant flower-garden, and a portion of a noble stone terrace, lying beneath one side of the many-turreted house. He stood entranced by the beauty of the scene, and, after a few moments, felt in his pocket for pencil and paper, in order to sketch it. He found both, and looking round him, saw a piece of the trunk of a felled tree, not yet removed by the care of the forester.

"A capital place to sketch from," thought George, as he folded his coat, and laid it upon the convenient block, and immediately became absorbed in his occupation. He was proceeding rapidly with his sketch, and feeling rather disposed to get it finished as quickly as he could, in order that he might return to the inn and procure some food, of which he stood in considerable need, when he caught the sound of galloping upon the turf in the distance behind him. He raised his head and lis-

tened; there it was, the dull rapid thud of hoofs on
the grass. Was there one rider, or were there
more? He listened again—only one, he thought;
and now the rapid noise ceased, and was succeeded
by the slow, pattering sound of a horse ridden daintily
and gently about and about, guided by a capricious
fancy. Still George listened, and presently there
came riding out of the shadowy distance into the
full expanse of the glade, down which the declining
sun sent golden rays, as if in salutation, a lady, who
was, as his first glance showed him, young and
beautiful. She was quite unconscious of his presence, for the piece of timber on which he had been
sitting was out of the line of sight, and though he
had risen, he was still standing beside it. She came
towards him, her slight form swaying to the movements of her bright bay thorough-bred, as she put
the animal through all sorts of fanciful paces, now
checking him with the rein, now encouraging him
with her clear sweet young voice, and patting
his arched neck with her white-gloved hand. The
young man looked out from his hiding-place, en-
raptured, as she came on, a vision of youth, beauty,
and refinement, down the wide green glade,

the sun shining on her, the birds singing, the flowers blooming for her, the proud walls of the old house rising grandly in the background, as if in boast of the worthy shelter that awaited her. Nearer and nearer she came, and now George Dallas could see her face distinctly, and could hear the pretty words with which she coaxed her horse. It was a face to remember; a face to be the happier for having seen; a face whose beauty was blended of form and colour, of soul, feature, and expression; a face which had all that the earth has to give of its best and fairest, touched with the glory which is higher and better, which earth has not to bestow. It was the face of a girl of nineteen, whose clear eyes were of golden brown, whose cheeks bloomed with the purest, most varying flower-like colour, whose rich golden hair shone in the sunlight, as its braids rippled and turned about with the movement of her head, tossed childishly to the rhythmical measure of her horse's tread.

Half a dozen trees only intervened between her and the spot where George Dallas stood, greedily watching her every movement and glance, when she took her hat off, and pushed the heavy golden hair off her broad white forehead. At that moment her horse jerked the rein she held loosely, and pulled her slightly forward, the hat falling from her hand on the grass.

"Now see what you have done," she said, with a gay laugh, as the animal stood still and looked foolish. "I declare I'll make you pick it up with your mouth. There, sir, turn, I tell you; come, you know how." And she put the horse through all the pretty tricks of stooping and half kneeling, in which she evidently felt much more pleasure than he did. But she did not succeed: he obeyed touch and word readily; but he did not pick up the hat. At last she desisted, and said with a funny look of mock patience:

"Very well, Sir Lancelot, if you won't you won't, so I must get off." She had just gathered her skirt in her hand, and was about to spring from her saddle, when George Dallas stepped out from among the trees, picked up the hat, and handed it to her, with a bow.

The young lady looked at him in astonishment, but she thanked him with self-possession, which he was far from sharing, and put her hat on, while Sir Lancelot pawed impatiently.

"Thank you," she said; "I did not see any one near."

"I was sitting yonder," said George, pointing to the spot whence he had emerged, "on some fallen timber, and was just taking the liberty of sketching the view of the house, when you rode up."

She coloured, looked pleased and interested, and said, hesitatingly, having bidden Sir Lancelot "stand :" "You are an artist, sir?"

"No," he answered, "at least, only in a very small way; but this is such a beautiful place, I was tempted to make a little sketch. But I fear I am intruding; perhaps strangers are not admitted."

"O yes, they are," she replied hurriedly. "We have not many strangers in this neighbourhood; but they are all welcome to come into the park, if they like. Had you finished your sketch?" she asked timidly, with a look towards the sheet of paper, which had fallen when Dallas rose, and had been fluttered into sight by the gentle wind. George saw the look, and caught eagerly at any pretext for prolonging the interview a few moments.

"May I venture to show you my poor attempt?" he asked, and without awaiting her answer, he stepped quickly back to the place he had left. The girl walked her horse gently forward, and as he stooped for the paper, she was beside him, and, lifting his head, he caught for a moment the full placid gaze of her limpid eyes. He reddened under the look, full of gentleness and interest as it was, and a pang shot through his heart, with the swift thought, that once he might have met such a woman as this on equal terms, and might have striven with the highest and the proudest for her favour. That was all over now; but at least he, even he, might sun himself in the brief light of her presence. She laid the rein on Sir Lancelot's neck, and took the little drawing from his hand with a timid expression of thanks.

"I am no judge," she said, when she had looked at it, and he had looked at her, his whole soul in his eyes; "but I think it is very nicely done. Would you not like to finish it? Or perhaps there are some other points of view you would like to take? I am sure my uncle, Sir Thomas Boldero, would be delighted to give you every facility. He is very fond of art, and—and takes a great interest in artists."

"You are very kind," said Dallas. "I shall be at Amherst a day or two longer, and I will take the liberty of making a few sketches—that splendid group of sycamores, for instance."

"Ah, yes," she said, laughing, "I call them the godfathers and godmothers of the park. They would make a pretty picture. I tried to draw them once, myself, but *you* cannot imagine what a mess I made of it."

"Indeed," said Dallas, with a smile, "and why am I to be supposed unable to imagine a failure?"

"Because you are an artist," she said, with charming archness and simplicity, "and, of course, do everything well."

This simple exhibition of faith in artists amused Dallas, to whom this girl was a sort of revelation of the possibilities of beauty, innocence, and *naïveté*.

"Of course," he replied gravely; "nevertheless I fear I shall not do justice to the sycamores."

And now came an inevitable pause, and he expected she would dismiss him and ride away, but she did not. It was not that she had any of the awkward want of manner which makes it difficult to terminate a chance interview, for she was perfectly graceful and self-possessed, and her manner was as far removed from clumsiness as from boldness. The girl was thinking, during the pause whose termination Dallas dreaded. After a little, she said:

"There is a very fine picture-gallery at the Sycamores, and I am sure it would give my uncle great pleasure to show it to you. Whenever any gentlemen from London are staying at Amherst, or passing through, Mr. Page at the inn tells them about the picture-gallery, and they come to see it, if they care about such things; perhaps it was he who told you?"

"No," said Dallas, "I am not indebted for the pleasure—for the happiness—of this day to Mr. Page. No one guided me here, but I happened to pass the gate, and a very civil old gentleman, who was doing some gardening at the lodge, asked me in."

His looks said more than his words dared to express, of the feelings with which his chance visit had inspired him. But the girl did not see his looks; she was idly playing with Sir Lancelot's mane, and thinking.

"Well," she said at last, settling herself in the saddle in a way unmistakably preliminary to departure, "if you would like to see the picture-gallery, and will walk round that way, through those trees, to the front of the house" —she pointed out the direction with the handle of her riding-whip—"I will go on before, and tell my uncle he is about to have a visitor to inspect his treasures."

"You are very kind," said Dallas earnestly, "and you offer me a very great pleasure. But Sir Thomas Boldero may be engaged—may think it an intrusion."

"And a thousand other English reasons for not accepting at once a civility frankly offered," said the girl, with a delightful laugh. "I assure you, I could not gratify my uncle more than by picking up a stray connoisseur; or my aunt than by bringing to her a gentleman of sufficient taste to admire her trees and flowers."

"And her niece, *Miss Carruthers*," thought George Dallas.

"So pray go round to the house. Don't forget your coat. I see it upon the ground—there. It has got rubbed against the damp bark, and there's a great patch of green upon it."

"That's of no consequence," said George gaily; "it's only an Amherst coat, and no beauty."

"You must not make little of Amherst," said the girl, with mock gravity, as George stood rubbing the green stain off his coat with his handkerchief; "we regard the town here as a kind of metropolis, and have profound faith in the shops and all to be purchased therein. Did dear old Evans make that coat?"

"A venerable person of that name sold it me," returned George, who had now thrown the coat over his arm, and stood, hat in hand, beside her horse.

"The dear! I should not mind letting him make me a habit," she said. "Good-bye, for the present—that way," again she pointed with her whip, and then cantered easily off, leaving George

in a state of mind which he would have found it
very difficult to define, so conflicting were his
thoughts and emotions. He looked after her,
until the last flutter of her skirt was lost in the
distance, and then he struck into the path which
she had indicated, and pursued it, musing.

"And that is Clare Carruthers! I thought
I had seen that head before, that graceful neck,
that crown of golden hair. Yes, it is she; and
little she thinks whom she is about to bring into
her uncle's house—the outcast and exile from
Poynings! I will see it out; why should I not?
I owe nothing to Carruthers that I should avoid
this fair, sweet girl, because he chooses to banish
me from her presence. What a presence it is!
What am I that I should come into it?" He
paused a moment, and a bitter tide of remembrance and self-reproach rushed over him, almost
overwhelming him. Then he went on more
quickly, and with a flushed cheek and heated
brow, for anger was again rising within him.
"You are very clever as well as very obstinate, my
worthy step-father, but you are not omnipotent
yet. Your darling niece, the beauty, the heiress,

the great lady, the treasure of price to be kept from the sight of me, from the very knowledge of anything so vile and lost, has met me, in the light of day, not by any device of mine, and has spoken to me, not in strained, forced courtesy, but of her own free will. What would you think of that, I wonder, if you knew it! And my mother? If the girl should ask my name, and should tell my mother of her chance meeting with a wandering artist, one Paul Ward, what will my mother think?—my dear conscientious mother, who has done for me what wounds her conscience so severely, and who will feel as if it were wounded afresh by this accidental meeting, with which she has nothing in the world to do." He lifted his hat, and fanned his face with it. His eyes were gleaming, his colour had risen; he looked strong, daring, active, and handsome—a man whom an innocent girl, all unlearned in life and in the world's ways, might well exalt in her guileless fancy into a hero, and be pardoned her mistake by older, sadder, and wiser heads.

"How beautiful she is, how frank, how graceful, how unspeakably innocent and refined! She

spoke to me with such an utter absence of conventional pretence, without a notion that she
might possibly be wrong in speaking to a stranger,
who had offered her a civility in her uncle's
park. She told that man on the balcony that
night that Sir Thomas Boldero was her uncle.
I did not remember it when the old man mentioned the name. How long has she been here, I
wonder? Is she as much here as at Poynings?
How surprised she would be if she knew that I
know who she is; that I have heard her voice
before to-day; that in the pocket-book she held
in her hand a few minutes ago there lies a
withered flower, which she once touched and
wore. Good God! What would a girl like that
think of me, if she knew what I am—if she knew
that I stole like a thief to the window of my
mother's house, and looked in, shivering, a poverty-stricken wretch, come there to ask for alms,
while she herself glittered among my mother's
company, like the star of beauty and youth she
is? How could she but despise me if she knew
it! But she will never know it, or me, most
likely. I shall try to get away and *work out all*

this, far away in a country where no memories of
sin and shame and sorrow will rise up around me
like ghosts. I am glad to have seen and spoken
to Clare Carruthers; it must do me good to
remember that such a woman really exists, and is
no poet's or romancer's dream. I am glad to
think of her as my mother's friend, companion,
daughter almost. My mother, who never had a
daughter, and has, God help her, no son *but me!*
But I shall never see her again, most likely.
When I reach the house, I shall find a pompous
servant, no doubt, charged with Sir Thomas's
compliments, and orders to show me round a
gallery of spurious Dutch pictures, copies of
Raphael and Carlo Dolce, and a lot of languish-
ing Lelys and gluttony-suggesting Knellers."

With these disparaging words in his thoughts,
George Dallas reached the border of the park,
and found himself in front of the house. The
façade was even more imposing and beautiful
than he had been led to expect by the distant
view of it, and the wide arched doorway gave
admittance to an extensive quadrangle beyond.
A stone terrace stretched away at either side of

the entrance, as at Poynings. Standing on the lower step, a tame peacock displaying his gaudy plumage by her side, he saw Miss Carruthers. She came forward to meet him with a heightened colour and an embarrassed manner, and said:

"I am very sorry, indeed, but Sir Thomas and my aunt are not at home. They had no intention of leaving home when I went out for my ride, but they have been gone for some time." She looked towards a servant who stood near, and added: "I am so sorry; nothing would have given my uncle more pleasure; but if you will allow me, I will send—"

George interrupted her, but with perfect politeness.

"Thank you very much, but, if you will allow me, I will take my leave, and hope to profit by Sir Thomas Boldero's kindness on a future occasion." He bowed deeply, and was turning away, when, seeing that she looked really distressed, he hesitated.

"I will show you the pictures myself, if you will come with me," she said, in a tone so frank, so kindly and engaging, that the sternest critic of manners in existence, supposing that critic to have been any other than an old maid, could not have condemned the spontaneous courtesy as forwardness. "I am an indifferent substitute for my uncle, as a cicerone, but I think I know the names of all the artists, and where all the pictures came from. Stephen,"—she spoke now to the servant,—"I am going to take this gentleman through the picture-gallery; go on before us if you please."

So George Dallas and Clare Carruthers entered the house together, and lingered over the old carvings in the hall, over their inspection of the sporting pictures which adorned it, and the dining-room, over the family portraits in the vestibule, the old china vases, and the rococo furniture. Every subject had an interest for them, and they did not think of asking themselves in what that interest originated and consisted. The girl did not know the young man's name, but his voice was full of the charm of sweet music for her, and in his face her fancy read strange and beautiful things. He was an

artist, she knew already, which in sober language
meant that she had seen a very tolerable sketch
which he had made. He was a poet, she felt
quite convinced; for did he not quote Tennyson, and Keats, and Coleridge, and even Herrick
and Herbert, as they wandered among the really
fine and valuable paintings which formed Sir
Thomas Boldero's collection, so aptly and with
such deep feeling and appreciation as could spring
only from a poetic soul?

It was the old story, which has never been
truly told, which shall never cease in the telling.
Both were young, and one was beautiful; and
though the present is an age which mocks at
love at first sight, and indeed regards love at all,
under any circumstances, with only decent toleration, not by any means amounting to favour,
it actually witnesses it sometimes. The young
man and the girl—the idle, dissolute, perverted
young man; the beautiful, pure, innocent, proud,
pious young girl—talked together that spring
afternoon, as the hours wore on to evening, of
art, of literature, of music, of travel, of the
countless things over which their fancy rambled,

and which had wondrous charms for her bright intellect and her secluded life, simple and ignorant in the midst of its luxury and refinement. All that was best and noblest in George's mind came out at the gentle bidding of the voice that sounded for him with a new, undreamed-of music; and the hard, cold, wicked world in which he lived, in which hitherto, with rare intervals of better impulses, he had taken delight, fell away from him, and was forgotten. The girl's grace and beauty, refinement and gentleness, were not more conspicuous than her bright intelligence and taste, cultivated, not indeed by travel or society, but by extensive and varied reading. Such was the influence which minute after minute was gaining upon George. And for her? Her fancy was busily at work too. She loved art; it filled her with wonder and reverence. Here was an artist, a young and handsome artist, of unexceptionable manners. She adored poetry, regarding it as a divine gift; and here was a poet—yes, a poet; for she had made Dallas confess that he very often wrote "verses;" but that was his modesty: she knew he wrote poetry—beautiful poetry. Would he ever let her see any of it?

"Yes, certainly," he had answered; "when I am famous, and there is a brisk competition for me among the publishers, I will send a copy of my poems to you."

"To me! But you do not know my name."

"O yes I do. You are Miss Carruthers."

"I am; but who told you?"

The question disconcerted Dallas a little. He turned it off by saying, "Why, how can you suppose I could be at Amherst without learning that the niece of Sir Thomas Boldero, of the Sycamores, is Miss Carruthers?"

"Ah, true; I did not think of that," said Clare simply. "But I do not live here generally; I live with another uncle, my father's brother—Sir Thomas is my mother's—Mr. Capel Carruthers, at Poynings, seven miles from here. Have you heard of Poynings?"

Yes, Mr. Dallas had heard of Poynings; but now he must take his leave. It had long been too dark to look at the pictures, and the young people were standing in the great hall, near the open door, whence they could see the gate and the archway, and a cluster of servants idling about and looking out for the return of the carriage. Clare was suddenly awakened to a remembrance of the lateness of the hour, and at once received her visitor's farewell, gracefully reiterating her assurances that her uncle would gladly make him free of the park for sketching purposes. She would tell Sir Thomas of the pleasant occurrences of the day;—by the bye, she had not the pleasure of knowing by what name she should mention him to her uncle.

"A very insignificant one, Miss Carruthers. My name is Paul Ward."

And so he left her, and, going slowly down the great avenue among the beeches, met a carriage containing a comely, good-humoured lady and an old gentleman, also comely and good-humoured; who both bowed and smiled graciously as he lifted his hat to them.

"Sir Thomas and my lady, of course," thought George; "a much nicer class of relatives than Capel Carruthers, I should say."

He walked briskly towards the town. While

he was in Clare's company he had forgotten how
hungry he was, but now the remembrance returned with full vigour, and he remembered very
clearly how many hours had elapsed since he had
eaten. When he came in sight of the railway-
station, a train was in the act of coming in from
London. As he struck into a little by-path leading to the inn, the passengers got out of the carriages, passed through the station gate, and began
to straggle up in the same direction. He and
they met where the by-path joined the road, and
he reached the inn, in the company of three of
the passengers, who were about to remain at
Amherst. Mr. Page was in the hall, and asked
George if he would dine.

"Dine?" said George. "Certainly. Give
me anything you like, so that you don't keep me
waiting; that's the chief thing."

"It *is* late, sir, indeed," remarked Mr. Page;
"half-past seven, sir."

"So late?" said George carelessly, as he turned
into the coffee-room.

CHAPTER VIII.

GLAMOUR.

WHEN George Dallas had dined, he left the coffee-room, and retired to the bedroom which he had ordered, and which looked refreshingly clean and comfortable, when mentally contrasted with the dingy quarters on which he had turned his back in the morning. It was yet early in the evening, but he was tired; tired by the excitement and the various emotions of the day, and also by the long hours passed in the fresh balmy country air, which had a strange soporific effect on a man whose lungs and limbs were of the town, towny. The evening air was still a little sharp, and George assented readily to the waiter's proposition, made when he perceived that no more orders for drink were to be elicited from the silent and preoccupied young man, that "a bit of fire" should be kindled in his room. Over that "bit of fire" he sat long, his arms folded on his breast, his head bent, his brow lowering, his eyes fixed on the glowing embers. Was he looking at faces in the fire—his parents' faces, the faces of friends, whom he had treated as enemies, of enemies whom he had taken for friends? Were reproachful eyes looking at him from out the past; were threatening glances in the present flashed on him? He sat there, black and moody, a long while, but at length his fixed gaze relaxed, the muscles of his mouth softened, broke into a slow smile, and a light came into his dull gloomy eyes. Then he rose, took his pocket-book from his breast-pocket, made some memoranda at the back of the sketch taken that day in Sir Thomas Boldero's park, put back the book, and, once more settling himself near the fire, lighted his pipe and began to smoke.

The musing look remained upon his face, but it was no longer painful, and, as he smoked, he fell to building castles in the air, as baseless, maybe, as the vapour which curled in fantastic wreaths about his face, but tenanted by hope, and inspired by higher and better resolves than had animated George Dallas for many a day. The twin angels,

love and gratitude, were near him; invisibly their
soft white wings were fluttering about him, refreshing the jaded heart and the stained brow.
His mother, and the girl whom he had that day
seen for the second time, and recognised with
feelings full of a bitter and evil impulse at first,
but who had soon exercised over him a nameless
fascination full of a pure and thrilling delight,
such as no pleasure of all his sin-stained life had
ever previously brought him—of these two he
was thinking. If George Dallas could have seen
his mother at the moment, when he, having laid
his exhausted pipe upon the little wooden chim-
neypiece, and hastily undressed, lay down in his
bed, with his hands clasped over the top of his
head, in his favourite attitude when he had anything particular to think of, he would have found
her not only thinking but talking of him. Mr.
Carruthers was absent, so was Clare; she had the
grand stately house all to herself, and she improved the occasion by having tea in her dressing-room, having dismissed her maid, affianced to
a thriving miller in the village, to a *tête-à-tête*
with her lover, and summoning her trusty friend

Mrs. Brookes to a confidential conference with her. The two women had no greater pleasure or pain in their lives than talking of George. There had been many seasons before and since her second marriage when Mrs. Carruthers had been obliged to abstain from mentioning him, so keen and terrible was her suffering on his account, and at such seasons Ellen Brookes had suffered keenly too, though she had only vaguely known wherefore, and had always waited until the thickest and darkest of the cloud had passed, and her mistress had once more summoned courage to broach the subject never absent from the mind of either.

There was no reticence on this occasion; the mother had taken a dangerous step, and one whose necessity she indeed deeply deplored, but she had gotten over the first great effort and the apprehension connected with it, and now she thought only of her son, she dwelt only upon the hope, the confidence, the instinctive belief within her, that this was really the turning-point, that her prayers had been heard, that the rock of a hard and stubborn heart had been struck and had yielded, that her son would turn from the old evil paths, would consider his ways and be wise for the future. So she sat and talked to the humble friend who knew her and loved her better than any one else in the world knew or loved her; and when she at length dismissed her and lay down to rest, there was more peace at her heart than had dwelt there for a long time past.

So one of the women of whom the prodigal son had thought gently and gratefully that night, was thinking of him with love that no unworthiness could kill or lesson, with hope which no experience could exhaust. And the other? Well, the other was playing and singing to her uncle and aunt in the green drawing-room at the Sycamores, and if she had said little to Sir Thomas and Lady Boldero concerning the young artist who was so delighted with the picture-gallery, and who had despaired of doing justice to the grand old trees in the park, it is presumable that, like the parrot of old renown, she thought the more.

George Dallas slept well that night in the little country inn, and awoke to a pleasant consciousness of rest, leisure, and expectation. As he dressed himself slowly, listening to the queer mixture of town and country sounds which arose inside and outside the house, he took up a similar train of thought to that in which sleep had interrupted him on the previous night, and began to form resolutions and to dream dreams. After he had breakfasted, and perused all the daily intelligence which found its way to Amherst, where the population were not remarkably eager for general information, and the *Illustrated London News* was represented by one copy, taken in by the clergyman's wife, and circulated among her special friends and favourites, he went out, and once more took the direction of the Sycamores.

Should he go into the park, he asked himself, or would that be too intrusive a proceeding? Sir Thomas, on his fair niece's showing, was evidently an elderly gentleman of kindly impulses, and who could say but that he might send a message to Mr. Page the landlord, inviting him to inform the stranger within his gates that he might have another look at the picture-gallery at the Sycamores? Was this a very wild idea? He did not know. It seemed to him as likely as not that a jolly kindly man, disposed to let his fellow-creatures enjoy a taste of the very abundant good things which providence had lavished on himself, might do a thing of the kind. A pompous, purse-proud, egotistical old fellow, who would regard every man unpossessed of landed property as a wretched creature, beneath his notice in all respects, except that of being made to admire and envy him as deeply as possible, might also think of sending such an invitation, but George Dallas felt quite sure Sir Thomas Boldero was not a man of that description. Suppose such a message should come? He had not given any name at the inn; he wished now he had done so; he would only take a short walk, and return to correct the inadvertence. At so early an hour there would be no likelihood of his seeing Miss Carruthers. It was in the afternoon she had ridden out yesterday, perhaps she would do the same to-day. At all events, he would return to the Sycamores on the chance, at the same hour as that at which he had seen her yesterday, and try his luck.

The road on which he was walking was one of the beautiful roads common in the scenery of

England, a road which dipped and undulated, and wound about and about, making the most of the natural features of the landscape without any real sacrifice of the public convenience, a road sha-dowed frequently by tall stately trees, and along one side of which the low park paling, with a broad belt of plantation beyond, which formed the boun-dary of the Sycamores, stretched for three miles. On the other side, a well-kept raised pathway ran alongside a hedge, never wanting in the succes-sive beauties of wild flowers and "tangle," and which furnished shelter to numerous birds. The day was bright and cheerful, and a light breeze was stirring the budding branches and lending a sense of exhilaration to the young man who so rarely looked on the fair face of nature, and who had unhappily had all his purer tastes and sym-pathies so early deadened. They revived under the influence of the scene and the softening effect of the adventure which had befallen him the day before. He stopped opposite the oaken gates, which had lain open yesterday, but were closed to-day, and he rambled on, further away from the town, and crossing the road, took his way along the park paling, where the fragrant odour from the shrubberies added a fresh pleasure to his walk.

He had passed a bend of the road which swept away from the large gates of the park, and was peering in at the mossy tufts, studded with violets and bluebells clustering round the stems of the young trees in the plantation, when his eyes lighted on a small gate, a kind of wicket in the paling, imperfectly secured by a very loose latch, and from which a straight narrow path, bordered with trimly-kept rows of ground ivy, led into a broader road dividing the plantation from the park.

"A side entrance, of course," said Dallas to himself, and then, looking across the road, he saw that just opposite the little gate there was a wooden stile, by which a path through the fields, leading, no doubt, into the town of Amherst, could be attained from the raised footpath.

"I suppose the land on both sides belongs to Sir Thomas," thought Dallas, and as he made a momentary pause, a large black Newfoundland dog, carrying a basket in his mouth, came down

the narrow path, bumped himself against the
loosely fastened gate, swung it open, and stopped
in the aperture, with a droll air of having done
something particularly clever. Dallas looked ad-
miringly at the beautiful creature, who was young,
awkward, and supremely happy, and the next instant he heard a voice speaking from the top of
the straight walk.

"Here, Cæsar," it said; "come here, sir; who
told you I was going that way?"

Cæsar tossed up his head, somewhat to the
detriment of the basket, and lolloped about with
his big black legs, but did not retrace his steps, and
the next moment Miss Carruthers appeared. A
few yards only divided her from George, who
stood outside the gate, his face turned full towards
her as she came down the path, and who promptly
took off his hat. She returned his salutation with
embarrassment, but with undisguisable pleasure,
and blushed most becomingly.

"I suppose I ought to walk on and leave her;
but I won't," said George to himself, in the momentary silence which followed their mutual salutation, and then, in a kind of desperation, he said:

"I am fortunate to meet you again, by a lucky accident, Miss Carruthers. You are out earlier to-day, and this is Cæsar's turn."

He patted the shiny black head of the Newfoundland, who still obstructed the entrance to the path, as he spoke, and Cæsar received the attention tolerably graciously.

"Yes, I generally walk early, and ride in the afternoon."

"Escorted by your dumb friends only," said George, in a tone not quite of interrogation.

Miss Carruthers blushed again, as she replied :

"Yes, my horse and my dog are my companions generally. My aunt never walks, and Sir Thomas never rides. Were you going into the park again, Mr. Ward ?"

By this time Cæsar had run out into the road, and was in a state of impatient perplexity, and evidently much inconvenienced by the basket, which he was too well trained to drop, but shook disconsolately as he glanced reproachfully at Clare, wondering how much longer she meant to keep him waiting.

"No, Miss Carruthers, I was merely walking

past the Sycamores, and recalling yesterday's pleasure—half gladly, half sadly, as I fancy we recall all pleasures."

"I—I told my uncle of your visit yesterday, and he said he was sorry to have missed you, and hoped you would see as much of the park as you liked. Did — did you finish your sketch, Mr. Ward? O, that horrid Cæsar, he will have the handle off my basket. Just see how he is knocking it against the stile."

She came hurriedly through the open gateway into the road, George following her.

"May I take it from him?" he said.

"O, pray do; there now, he is over the stile, and running through the field."

George rushed away in pursuit of Cæsar, triumphant at his success in thus terminating a period of inaction for which he saw no reasonable excuse. Miss Carruthers mounted the stile in a more leisurely fashion, turned into the footpath which led through the field, and in a few moments met George returning, her basket in his hand, and Cæsar slouching along beside him, sulky and discontented.

She thanked George, told him she was going
nearly as far as Amherst by the "short cut,"
which lay through her uncle's land, and the two
young people in another minute found themselves
walking side by side, as if such an arrangement
were quite a matter of course, to which Mrs.
Grundy could not possibly make any objection.
Of course it was highly imprudent, not to say
improper, and one of the two was perfectly conscious alike of the imprudence and the impro-
priety; perfectly conscious, also, that both were
increased by the fact that he was George Dallas,
and the young lady was Clare Carruthers, the
niece of his step-father, the girl, on whose account
mainly he had been shut out from the house called
by courtesy his mother's. As for Clare Carruthers,
she knew little or nothing of life and the world of
observances and rules of behaviour. Sheltered from
the touch, from the breath, from the very knowledge of ill, the girl had always been free with a
frank innocent freedom, happy with a guileless
happiness, and as unsophisticated as any girl could
well be in this wide-awake realistic nineteenth century.   She was highly imaginative, emphatically

of the romantic temperament, and, in short, a
Lydia Languish without the caricature. Her
notions of literary men, artists, and the like, were
derived from their works; and as the little glimpse
which she had as yet had of society (she had only
"come out" at the ball at Poynings in February)
had not enabled her to correct her ideas by comparison with reality, she cherished her illusions
with ardour proportioned to their fallaciousness.
The young men of her acquaintance were of
either of two species: sons of country gentlemen,
with means and inclination to devote themselves
to the kind of life their fathers led, or military
magnificoes, of whom Clare, contrary to the fashion
of young ladies in general, entertained a mean and
contemptuous opinion. When Captain Marsh and
Captain Clitheroe were home " on leave," they
found it convenient and agreeable to pass a good
deal of their leisure at Poynings ; and as they
happened to be ninnies of the first magnitude,
whose insignificance in every sense worth mention was only equalled by their conceit, Miss Carruthers had conceived a prejudice against military
men in general, founded upon her dislike of the

two specimens with whom she was most familiar.
Clergymen are not uncommonly heroes in the imagination of young girls, but the most determined
curate-worshipper could not have invested the
clergymen who cured the souls in and about
Amherst with heroic qualities. They were three
in number. One was fat, bald, and devoted to
antiquarianism and port wine. Another was thin,
pock-marked, ill-tempered, deaf, and a flute-
player. The third was a magistrate, a fox-hun-
ter, and a despiser of womankind. In conclusion,
all three were married, and Miss Carruthers was
so unsophisticated, that, if they had been all three
as handsome and irresistible as Adonis, she would
never have thought of them in the way of mun-
dane admiration, such being the case. So Clare's
imagination had no home pasture in which to
feed, and roamed far afield.

It had taken its hue from her tastes, which
were strongly pronounced, in the direction of literature. Clare had received a "good education;"
that is to say, she had been placed by a fashionable mother under the care of a fashionable go-
verness, who had superintended fashionable mas-

ters while they imparted a knowledge of music, drawing, dancing, and a couple of modern languages to her pretty, docile, intelligent pupil. The more solid branches of instruction Clare had climbed under Miss Pettigrew's personal care, and had "done credit" to her instructress, as the phrase goes. But the upshot of it all was, that she had very little sound knowledge, and that the real educational process had commenced for her with the termination of Miss Pettigrew's reign, and had received considerable impetus when Clare had been transferred—on the not particularly lamented decease of the fashionable mother, who was Sir Thomas Boldero's sister, and remarkably unlike that hearty and unworldly country gentleman— to Poynings and the guardianship of Mr. Carruthers. Then the girl began to read after her own fancy indeed, unguided and uncontrolled, but in an omnivorous fashion; and as she was full of feeling, fancy and enthusiasm, her reading ran a good deal in the poetical, romantic, and imaginative line. Novels she devoured, and she was of course a devotee of Tennyson and Longfellow, saying of the latter, as her highest idea of praise, that she could hardly believe him to be an American, or a dweller in that odious vulgar country, and wondering why Mrs. Carruthers seemed a little annoyed by the observation. She read history, too, provided it was picturesquely written, and books of travel, exploration, and adventure she delighted in. Periodical literature she was specially addicted to, and it was rather a pleasant little vanity of Clare to "keep up with" all the serial stories—not confusing the characters or the incidents, no matter how numerous they were, and to know the tables of contents of all the magazines and reviews thoroughly. She had so much access to books that, as far as a lady's possible requirements could go, it might be said, without exaggeration, to be unlimited. Not only did the Sycamores boast a fine library, kept up with the utmost care and attention by Sir Thomas Boldero, and of which she had the freedom, but Poynings was also very creditably endowed in a similar respect, and Mrs. Carruthers, as persistent a reader as Clare, if less discursive, subscribed largely to Mudie's. Croquet had not yet assumed its sovereign sway over English young-persondom, and none but ponderous and formal hospitalities prevailed at Poynings, so that Clare had ample leisure to bestow upon her books, her pets, and her flowers. She was so surrounded with luxury and comfort, that it was not wonderful she should invest opposite conditions of existence with irresistible charms; and her habitual associates were so commonplace, so prosperous and conventional, that her aspirations for opportunities of heroworship naturally directed themselves towards oppressed worth, unappreciated genius, and fiery hearts struggling manfully with adverse fate. "The red planet Mars" was a great favourite with her, and to suffer and be strong a much finer idea to her mind than not to suffer and to have no particular occasion for strength. She knew little of the realities of life, having never had a deeper grief than that caused by the death of her mother, and she was in the habit of reproaching herself very bitterly with the superficiality and the insufficiency of the sorrow she had experienced on that occasion, and therefore mild and merciful judges would have pitied and excused her errors of judgment, her impulsive de-

parture from conventional rules. Mild and merciful judges are not plentiful commodities, however, and Mrs. Grundy would doubtless have had
a great deal to say, and a very fair pretext for
saying it, had she seen Miss Carruthers strolling
through the fields which lay between the Sycamores and Amherst, in deep and undisguisedly
delighted conversation with a strange young man,
who was apparently absorbed in the pleasure of
talking to and listening to her, while Cæsar trotted
now by the side of the one, anon of the other,
with serene and friendly complacency. Mrs.
Grundy was, however, not destined to know anything about the " very suspicious" circumstance
for the present. And George Dallas and Clare
Carruthers, with the unscrupulous yielding to the
impulse of the moment, which affords youth such
splendid opportunities for getting into scrapes,
from which the utmost efforts of their elders are
powerless to extricate them, walked and talked and
improved the shining hours into a familiar acquaintance, which the girl would have called
friendship, but which the young man felt, only
too surely, was love at first sight. He had mocked

at such an idea, had denied its existence, had de-
rided it with tongue and pen, but here it was,
facing him now, delivering to him a silent chal-
lenge to deny, dispute, or mock at it any more.

A faint suspicion that the beautiful girl whom
he had seen yesterday for the second time meant
something in his life, which no woman had ever
meant before, had hung about him since he had
left the Sycamores after their first interview; but
now, as he walked beside her, he felt that he had
entered the enchanted land, that he had passed
away from old things, and the chain of his old
life had fallen from him. For weal or woe, present with her or absent from her, he knew he
loved this girl, the one girl whom it was absolutely forbidden to him to love.

They had talked commonplaces at first, though
each was conscious that the flurried earnestness
of the other's manner was an absurd commentary
upon the ordinary style of their conversation.
George had asked, and Clare had implied, no permission for him to accompany her on her walk; he
had quietly taken it for granted, and she had as
quietly acquiesced, and it so happened that they

did not meet a single person to stare at the tall, gaunt-looking but handsome stranger walking with Miss Carruthers, to wonder who he "mought a bin," and proceed to impart his curiosity to the servants at the Sycamores, or the gossip at the alehouse.

"This path is not much used," said George.

"No, very little indeed," replied Clare. "You see it does not lead directly anywhere but to the Sycamores, and so the farming people, my uncle's servants, and tradespeople, back and forward to the park, chiefly use it. I often come this way and do not meet a soul."

"Are you going into the town?"

"Not all the way: just to the turnpike on the Poynings road. Do you know Mr. Carruthers's place, Mr. Ward?"

George felt rather uncomfortable as he answered in the negative, though it was such a small matter, and the false statement did not harm anybody. He had told a tolerable number of lies in the course of his life, but he shrank with keen and unaccustomed pain from making this girl, whose golden brown eyes looked at him so frankly, whose sweet face beamed on him so innocently, a false answer.

"I am going to the cottage on the roadside, just below the turnpike," Clare continued; "an old servant of my aunt lives there, and I have a message from her. I often go to see her, not so much from kindness, I'm afraid, as because I hate to walk outside the park without an object."

"And you don't mind riding without an escort any more than you do walking without one," said George, not in the tone of a question, but in that of a simple remark. Clare looked at him with some surprise; he met the look with a meaning smile.

"You dislike the attendance of a groom, Miss Carruthers, and never admit it except in case of necessity. You are surprised, I see: you will be still more surprised when I tell you I learned this, not from seeing you ride alone in the park—there is nothing unusual in that, especially when you are on such good terms with your horse—but from your own lips."

"From my own lips, what can you possibly mean, Mr. Ward? I never saw you until yesterday, and I know I never mentioned the subject then."

The young man drew imperceptibly nearer to her, on the narrow path where they were walking, and as he spoke the following sentences, he took from his breast-pocket a little note-case, which he held in his left hand, at which she glanced curiously once or twice.

"You saw me for the first time yesterday, Miss Carruthers, but I had seen you before. I had seen you the centre of a brilliant society, the pride and belle of a ball-room where I had no place." ("Now," thought George, "if she only goes home and tells my mother all this, it will be a nice business. Never mind, I can't help it;" and he went on impetuously.) The girl made no remark, but she looked at him with growing astonishment. "You talked to a gentleman happier than I—for he was with you—of your daily rides, and I heard all you said. Forgive me, the first tone of your voice told me it was but a light and trivial conversation, or I would not have listened to it." (George is not certain that he is telling the truth here, but she is convinced of it; for is he not an author, an artist, a hero?) "I even heard the gentleman's name with whom you were talking, and just before you passed out of my hearing you unconsciously gave me *this*."

He opened the note-book, took out a folded slip of paper, opened that too, and held towards Clare, but without giving it into her hand, a slip of myrtle.

"*I* gave you that, Mr. Ward!" she exclaimed. "*I*—when—where—how? What do you mean? I remember no such conversation as you describe; I don't remember anything about a ball or a piece of myrtle. When and where was it? I have been out so little in London."

Now George had said nothing about London, but opportunely remembering that he could not explain the circumstances he had rather rashly mentioned, and that, unexplained, they might lead her to the conclusion that the part he had played on the mysterious occasion in question had been that of a burglar, he adroitly availed himself of her error. True, on the other hand, she might very possibly think that the only part which a spectator at a ball in London, who was not a par-

taker in its festivities, could have played must
have been that of a waiter, which was not a pleasant suggestion; but somehow he felt no apprehension on that score. The girl went on eagerly
questioning him, but he only smiled, very sweetly
and slowly, as he carefully replaced the withered twig
in the note-book, and the note-book in his pocket.

"I cannot answer your questions, Miss Carruthers; *this is my secret*—a cherishèd one, I
assure you. The time may come, though the
probability is very dim and distant just now, when
I shall tell you when, and where, and how I saw
you first; and if ever that time should come," he
stopped, cleared his voice, and went on, "things
will be so different with me that I shall have nothing to be ashamed or afraid of."

"*Ashamed* of, Mr. Ward?" said Clare, in a
sweet soft tone of deprecating wonder. All her
curiosity had been banished by the trouble and
sadness of his manner, and profound interest and
sympathy had taken its place.

"You think I ought not to use that word; I
thank you for the gentle judgment," said George,
his manner indescribably softened and deepened;

"but if ever I am in a position to tell you—but why do I talk such nonsense? I am only a waif, a stray, thrown for a moment in your path, to be swept from it the next and forgotten."

This was dangerous ground, and they both felt it. A chance meeting, a brief association which perhaps never ought to have been; and here was this girl, well brought up, in the strictest sense of the term, yielding to the dangerous charm of the stranger's society, and feeling her heart die within her as his words showed the prospect before her. Her complexion died too, for Clare's was a tell-tale face, on which emotion had irresistible power. George saw the sudden paleness, and she knew he saw it.

"I—I hope not," she said, rather incoherently. "I—I think not. You are an artist and an author, you know." (How ashamed George felt, how abashed in the presence of this self-deluding innocence of hers!) "And I, as well as all the world, shall hear of you."

"*You*, as well as all the world," he repeated, in a dreamy tone. "Well, perhaps so. I will try to think so, and to hope it will be——"

He stopped; the gentleman's nature in him still existing, still ready at call, notwithstanding his degradation, withheld him from presuming on the position in which he found himself, and in which the girl's innocent impulsiveness had placed her. To him, with his knowledge of who she was, and who he was, with the curious relation of severance which existed between them, the sort of intimacy which had sprung up, had not so much strangeness as it externally exhibited, and he had to remind himself that she did not share that knowledge, and therefore stood on a different level to his, in the matter. He determined to get off the dangerous ground, and there was a convincing proof in that determination that the tide had turned for the young man, that he had indeed resolved upon the better way. His revenge upon his step-father lay ready to his hand; the unconscious girl made it plain to him that he had excited a strange and strong interest in her. It was not a bad initiation of the prodigal's project of reform that he renounced that revenge, and turned away from the temptation to improve his chance advantage into the establishment of an

avowed mutual interest. This step he took by
saying, gaily, "Then I have your permission to
send you my first work, Miss Carruthers, and you
promise it a place in that grand old library I had
a glimpse of yesterday?"

A little shade of something like disappointment crossed Clare's sunny face. The sudden
transition in his tone jarred with her feelings of
curiosity, romance, and flattered vanity. For
Clare had her meed of that quality, like other
women and men, and had never had it so plea-
santly gratified as on the present occasion. But
she had too much good breeding to be pertinacious
on any subject, and too much delicacy of perception to fail in taking the hint which the alteration
in George's manner conveyed. So there was no
further allusion to the sprig of myrtle or to the
future probability of a disclosure; but the two
walked on together, and talked of books, pictures,
and the toils and triumphs of a literary life
(George, to do him justice, not affecting a larger
share in them than was really his), until they
neared Clare's destination. The footpath which
they had followed had led them by a gentle rise

in the ground to the brow of a little hill, similar
to that from which George had seen his mother's
carriage approach Amherst on the preceding day,
but from the opposite end of the town. Immediately under the brow of this hill, and approached
by the path, which inclined towards its trim green
gate, stood a neat small cottage, in a square bit of
garden, turning its red-brick vine-covered side to
the road beneath. When George saw this dwell-
ing, he knew his brief spell of enjoyment was over.

"That is the cottage," said Clare, and he had
the consolation of observing that there was no
particular elation in her voice or in her face.
"Sir Thomas built it for its present tenant."

"Shall you be going back to the Sycamores
alone, Miss Carruthers?" asked George, in the
most utterly irrelevant manner. He had a wild
notion of asking leave to wait for her, and escort
her home. Again Clare blushed as she replied
hurriedly:

"No, I shall not. My aunt is to pick me up
here in the carriage, on her way to the town, and
I return to Poynings this evening. I have been
away a fortnight."

George longed to question her concerning life at Poynings, longed to mention his mother's name, or to say something to the girl that would lead her to mention it; but the risk was too great, and he refrained.

"Indeed! and when do you return to the Sycamores?" was all he said.

"It is quite uncertain," she replied. "I fancy my uncle means to go to London for part of the season, but we don't quite know yet; he never says much about his plans." She stopped abruptly, as if conscious that she was not conveying a very pleasing impression of her uncle. George understood her, and correctly, to refer to Mr. Carruthers.

They had descended the incline by this time, and were close to the cottage gate. It lay open, and Cæsar ran up to the prim little green door.

"Come here, sir," called Clare; "please let him have the basket again, Mr. Ward. Old Willcox reared him for me, from a puppy, and he likes to see him at his tricks. Thank you. Now then, go on, Cæsar."

Her hand was on the open gate, her face turned away from the cottage, towards George— it was no easier to her to say good-bye than to him, he thought; but it must be said, so he began to say it.

"Then, Miss Carruthers, here I must leave you; and soon I must leave Amherst."

Perhaps he hoped she would repeat the invitation of yesterday. She did not; she only said:

"Thank you very much for your escort, Mr. Ward. Good-bye."

It was the coldest, most constrained of adieux. He felt it so, and yet he was not altogether dissatisfied; he would have been more so, had she retained the natural grace of her manner and the sweet gaiety of her tone. He would have given much to touch her hand at parting, but she did not offer it; but with a bow passed up the little walk to the cottage door, and in a moment the door had closed upon her, and she was lost to his sight.

He lingered upon the high road from which he could see the cottage, and gazed at the window, in the hope of catching another glimpse of

Clare; but suddenly remembering that she might perhaps see him from the interior of the room, and be offended by his doing so, he walked briskly away in a frame of mind hard to describe, and with feelings of a conflicting character. Above the tumult of new-born love, of pride, rage, mortification, anger, hope, the trust of youth in itself, and dawning resolutions of good, there was this thought, clear and prominent:

" If I am ever to see her again, it shall be in my own character, and by no tricky subterfuge. If she ever comes to care for me, she shall not be ashamed of me."

George Dallas returned to the inn, where his taciturnity and preoccupation did not escape notice by the waiters and Mr. Page, who accounted for it by commenting on his request for writing-materials, to the use of which he addressed himself in his own room, as a " hoddity of them literary gents; if they ain't blabby and blazin' drunk, they're most times uncommon sullen. This un's a poetical chap, I take it."

That evening George heard from his mother. She desired him to come to Poynings at twelve

o'clock on the following Monday (this was Thursday), and to wait in the shrubbery on the left of
the house until she should join him. The note
was brief, but affectionate, and of course made
George understand that she had received the
jewels.

Late in the afternoon of the day which had
witnessed her second interview with the young
man whom she knew as Paul Ward, and with
whom her girlish fancy was delightfully busy,
Clare Carruthers arrived at Poynings. She received an affectionate greeting from Mrs. Carruthers, inquired for her uncle, learned that no communication had been received from him that day,
and therefore his wife concluded that his original
arrangement to return on the following Tuesday
morning remained unaltered; and then went off
to see that Sir Lancelot, who had been brought
home from the Sycamores by a groom, was well
cared for. Somehow, the beautiful animal had a
deeper interest than ever for his young mistress.
She touched his silken mane with a lighter, more
lingering touch; she talked to him with a softer
voice.

"He did not forget to mention you," she whispered to the intelligent creature, as she held his small muzzle in one hand and stroked his face with the other. "I wonder, I wonder, shall we ever see him again."

When the two ladies were together in the drawing-room that evening, and the lamps were lighted, cheerful fires burning brightly in the two grates, which were none too many for the proportions of the noble room, the scene presented was one which would have suggested a confidential, cozy chat to the uninitiated male observer. But there was no chat and no confidence there that evening. Ordinarily, Mrs. Carruthers and Clare "got on" together very nicely, and were as thorough friends as the difference in their respective ages and the trouble in the elder lady's life, hidden from the younger, would permit. But each was a woman of naturally independent mind, and their companionship did not constrain either. Therefore the one sat down at a writing-table, and the other at the piano, without either feeling that the other expected to be talked to. Had not Mrs. Carruthers's preoccupation, her absorption in the hopes and fears which were all inspired by her son, so engrossed her attention, that she could not have observed anything not specially impressed upon her notice, she would have seen that Clare was more silent than usual, that her manner was absent, and that she had a little air of making music an excuse for thought. The leaves of her music-book were not turned, and her fingers strayed over the keys, in old melodies played almost unconsciously, or paused for many minutes of unbroken silence. She had not mentioned the incidents of the last two days to Mrs. Carruthers, not that she intended to leave them finally unspoken of, but that some undefined feeling prompted her to think them over first;—so she explained her reticence to herself.

While Clare played, Mrs. Carruthers wrote, and the girl, glancing towards her sometimes, saw that her face wore an expression of painful and intense thought. She wrote rapidly, and evidently at great length, covering sheet after sheet of foreign letter paper with bold firm characters, and once Clare remarked that she took a memorandum-book out of her pocket and consulted it. As she replaced the book, a slip of paper fluttered from between the leaves and fell to the ground, unobserved either by herself or Clare. Shortly afterwards Mrs. Carruthers rose, collected her papers into a loose heap upon the table, and left the room, still with the same preoccupied expression on her face. Clare went on playing for a few moments, then, finding Mrs. Carruthers did not return, she yielded to the sense of freedom inspired by finding herself alone, and leaving the piano, went over to one of the fireplaces and stood by the low mantelpiece, lost in thought. Several minutes passed away as she stood thus, then she roused herself, and was about to return to the piano, when her attention was attacted to a small slip of paper which lay on the floor near the writing-table. She picked it up, and saw written upon it two words only, but words which caused her an indescribable thrill of surprise. They were

Paul Ward.

"Mrs. Carruthers dropped this paper," said Clare to herself, "and *he* wrote the name. I know his hand, I saw it in the book he took the sketch in. Who is he? How does she know him? I wish she would return. I must ask her." But then, in the midst of her eagerness, Clare remembered a certain air of mystery about her chance acquaintance; she recalled the tone in which he had said, "That is my secret," the hints he had let fall that there existed something which time must clear up. She remembered, too, that he had not betrayed any acquaintance with Mrs. Carruthers, had not even *looked* like it when she had mentioned Poynings and her uncle (and Clare had a curiously distinct recollection of Mr. Paul Ward's looks); finally she' thought how—surely she might be said *to know*, so strongly and reasonably did she suspect—that there were trials and experiences in Mrs. Carruthers's life to which she held no clue, and perhaps this strange circumstance might be connected with them.

"It is *his* secret and *hers*, if she knows him," the girl thought, "and I shall best be true and loyal to them both by asking nothing, by seeking to know nothing, until I am told." And here a sudden thrill of joy, joy so pure and vivid that it should have made her understand her own feelings without further investigation, shot through the girl's heart, as she thought:

"If she knows him, my chance of seeing him again is much greater. In time I must come to understand it all."

So Clare allowed the paper to fall from her hands upon the carpet whence she had taken it, and when Mrs. Carruthers re-entered the room bringing a packet of letters which she had gone to seek, Clare had resumed her place at the piano.

CHAPTER IX.

It was the fifth morning after George Dallas's arrival in Amherst, the day on which his mother had appointed by letter for him to go over to Poynings, and there receive that which was to set him free from the incubus of debt and difficulty which had so long oppressed him. An anticipation of pleasure crossed his mind so soon as he first opened his eyes; he soon remembered whence the satisfaction sprung, and on going to the window and looking out, he found that nature and he were once again in accord. As at the time of his misery she had worn her blackest garb, her direst expression, so now, when hope seemed to gleam upon him, did nature don her flowery robes and array herself in her brightest verdant sheen. Spring was rapidly ripening into summer; into the clean and comely little town, which itself was radiant with whitened door-steps, and newly painted wood-

work, and polished brass fittings, came wafted
delicious odours from outlying gardens and uplands,
where the tossing grass went waving to and fro
like the undulations of a restless sea, and in the
midst of which the sturdy old farm-houses, dotted
here and there, stood out like red-faced islands.
Dust, which even the frequent April showers could
not lay, was blowing in Amherst streets; blinds,
which had been carefully laid by during the winter
(the Amherst mind had scarcely arrived at spring
blinds for outside use, and contented itself with
modest striped sacking, fastened between hooks on
the shop fronts, and poles socketed into the pavement), were brought forth and hung up in all the
glory of cleanliness. It was reported by those who
had been early astir, that Tom Leigh, the mail-
cart driver, had been seen with his white hat on
that morning, and any Amherstian who may have
previously doubted whether the fine weather had
actually arrived, must have been flinty-hearted
and obdurate indeed not to have accepted that
assurance.

The sunshine and the general brightness of the
day had its due effect on George Dallas, who was

young, for a nineteenth-century man almost romantic, and certainly impressible. His spirits rose
within him, as, his breakfast finished, he started off
to walk to Poynings. Drinking in the loveliness
of the broad sun-steeped landscape, the sweet odours
coming towards him on the soft breeze, the pleasant sound, were it chink of blacksmith's hammer,
or hum of bees, or voice of cuckoo hidden deep in
distant bright-leaved woods, the young man for a
time forgot his baser associations and seemed to
rise, in the surroundings of the moment, to a
better and purer frame of mind than he had known
for many years. Natural, under such circumstances, was the first turning of his thoughts to his
mother, to whose deep love and self-sacrifice he was
indebted for the freedom which at length was about
to be his. In his worst times there had been
one bright spot of love for her in all the black folly
of his life, and now the recollection of her disin-
terestedness and long suffering on his behalf made
her as purely dear to him as when, in the old days
that seemed so long ago, he had said his prayers
at her knee. He recollected walking with her in
their garden on mornings like these, when they

were all in all to each other, soon after his father's
death, when that chastening memory was on them
both, and before there was any thought of Mr. Carruthers or his niece—or his niece!—and straight-
way off went his thoughts into a different channel.
What a pretty girl! so soft and quiet, so fresh
withal, and frank, and guileless, so different from—
Well, he didn't know; with similar advantages
Harriet might have been very much the same.
But Miss Carruthers was certainly specially charming; the talk which they had had together showed
that. The talk which they had together? Was he
not entering her own domain? What if she were
to meet and recognise him there? That would spoil
all their plans. A word from her would—O no!
Though Mrs. Carruthers might not have been
intended as a conspirator by nature, George felt by
his recent experience of his mother's movements
that she would have sufficient foresight to prevent
Clare from leaving the house, just at that time,
lest she might discover the rendezvous in the
shrubbery. The tact that had so rapidly shifted
the venue of their last meeting from the bustle
of the draper's to the calm solitude of the dentist's

would assuredly be sufficient to prevent a young
girl from intruding on their next appointment.

Busy with these thoughts, and ever and anon
pausing to look round him at the fair scenes through
which he was passing, George Dallas pursued his
way along the high road until he gained the sum-
mit of the little hill whence is obtained the first
view of Poynings and its grounds. There he stopped suddenly; from that point he had always intended to reconnoitre, but he had never anticipated
seeing what he did see—a carriage driving through
the open lodge gates, and in the carriage reclining
at his ease no less a person than Mr. Capel Carruthers. It was he, not a doubt about it, in the
respectability of his glossy broad-brimmed hat, in
his white whiskers, in his close-fitting dogskin
gloves, in the very double gold eye-glass with which
he was looking at nature in a very patronising
manner. Even if he had not been short-sighted,
Mr. Carruthers was at such a distance as would
utterly have prevented him from recognising any
one on the top of the hill; but George Dallas no
sooner saw him than instinctively he crouched
down by the hedge-side and waited until the car-

riage was rolling down the avenue; then he slowly raised himself, muttering:

"What the deuce has brought him back just now? confound him! What on earth will she do? It's most infernally provoking, just at this very nick of time; he might have kept off a few hours longer. She won't come to the shrubbery now; she's frightened out of her life at that old ruffian, and, by George, I shall be put off again! After all I've said to Routh, after all the castles in the air which I've been building on the chance of getting free, I shall have to slink back to town empty-handed!" He was leaning over a gate in the hedge, and as he spoke he shook his fist at the unconscious county magistrate, visible in the distance now but by the crown of his hat. "Except," continued George, " knowing how deeply I'm involved, she'll risk all hazards and come to the shrubbery. Perhaps she's started now, not expecting him, and when he reaches the house and doesn't find her there—he's always hanging on her trail, curse him!—he will make inquiries and follow her. That would be worst of all, for not only should I miss what she promised me, but she would come to grief herself, poor darling. Well, I must chance it, whatever happens."

He turned down a by-lane which ran at right angles to the avenue, pursuing which he came upon a low park paling enclosing the shrubbery. Carefully looking round him, and finding no one within sight, he climbed the paling, and dropped noiselessly upon the primrose-decked bank on the other side. All quiet; nothing moving but the birds darting in and out among the bright green trees, and the grasshoppers in myriads round his feet. The walk had tired him, and he lay down on the mossy turf and awaited his mother's coming. Mossy turf, soft and sweet-smelling, the loud carol of the birds, the pleasant, soothing, slumberous sound of the trees bending gently towards each other as the mild air rustled in the leaves. It was long since he had experienced these influences, but he was now under their spell. What did they re-call? Boyhood's days; the Bishop's Wood, where they went birds'-nesting; Duke Primus, who wore "stick-ups," and was the cock of the school, and Charley Cope, who used to tell such good stories in bed, and Bergemann, a German boy, who was drowned in a pond in just such a part of the wood as this, and—twelve o'clock rings sharply out from the turret clock in Poynings stables, and at its sound away fly the ghosts of the past. Twelve o'clock, the time appointed in his mother's letter for him to meet her in that very spot. He rose up from the turf, and sheltering himself behind the broad trunk of an old tree, looked anxiously in the direction of the house. No human being was to be seen; a few rabbits whisked noiselessly about, their little white tails gleaming as they disappeared in the brushwood, but they and the birds and the grasshoppers comprised all the life about the place. He looked on the big trees and the chequered shade between them, and the glimpses of blue skylight between their topmost boughs; he left his vantage ground and strode listlessly to and fro; the quarter chime rung out from the turret, then the half hour, and still no one came.

Some one coming at last! George's quick eyes make out a female figure in the far distance, not his mother, though. This woman's back is bowed, her step slow and hesitating, unlike Mrs. Carruthers, on whose matronly beauty Time has as yet laid his gentlest touch. He must stand aside, he thought, amongst the trees until the new comer had passed by; but as the woman approached, her gait and figure seemed familiar to him, and when she raised her head and looked round her as though expecting some one, he recognised Nurse Brookes. The old woman gave a suppressed scream as George Dallas stepped out from among the trees and stood before her.

"I could not help it, George," said she; "I could not help it, though I was looking for and expecting you at that moment, and that's more than you were doing for me, isn't it? You were expecting some one else, my boy?"

"Is anything the matter? Is she ill? Has her husband found out?"

"Nothing! She's—well, as well as may be, poor dear, and——"

"Then she hasn't been able to do what she promised?"

"O, George, George, did you ever know her fail in doing what she promised, from the days when you were a baby until now? Better for her poor thing, as I've often told her, if she hadn't—"

"Yes, yes, nurse, I know all about that, of course; but why isn't she here now?"

"She daren't come, George. Master's come home unexpected, and he and Miss Clare are with her, and there is no chance for her to make an excuse to get away. So she just runs into her dressing-room for a minute, and sends to me—she always sends to me in her troubles, as you've seen many a time and oft, Master George—and tells me, she says, 'Take this and go into the shrubbery, and tell George,' she says, 'why I couldn't come, and that I sent it him with my heart's love, and God bless him,' she says."

As the old woman spoke, she produced from her pocket a round flat parcel wrapped in writing-paper, which she handed to Dallas. He took it with a very weak attempt at unconcern (he did not know with how much of their secret his mother might have intrusted the old nurse), and thrust it into his breast-pocket, saying at the same time, "Thanks, nurse. That's all right. Did she say anything else?"

"Nothing, I think. O yes—that of course now you would not remain in the neighbourhood, and that you were to be sure to write to her, and send your address."

"She need not be afraid—I'm off at once! Good-bye, nurse. Tell my mother I'll hold to all I promised her. Thank her a thousand times, bless her! Good-bye, dear old woman; perhaps the next time we meet I shan't have to skulk in a wood when I want to see my mother!"

He pressed a hasty kiss on the old woman's upturned face, and hurried away. The last sound he had uttered seemed to have rekindled the old vindictive feeling in his mind, for as he strode away he muttered to himself: "Skulking in a wood, hiding behind trees—a pretty way for a son to seek his mother, and she never to come after all! Prevented by her fear of that pompous idiot, her husband. To think of her, such as I recollect her, being afraid of an empty-headed dotard. And yet he is kind to her. She said so herself—that's nothing; but Nurse Brookes said so too—that's something—that's everything. If he were not— if he treated her badly—he should rue it. But he is fond of her, and proud of her, as well he may be; and Clare, that charming girl, is his niece. Charming, indeed! Ah, Capel Carruthers, you have a wholesome horror of me, but you little know that two guardian angels plead for you!"

The sight of the park paling over which he had climbed into the shrubbery, and over which lay his only way out of it, seemed to change the tenor of his thoughts. He stopped at once, and looking cautiously round, stepped in among the trees, and drew from his breast the packet which Nurse Brookes had given to him. He tore off the outer covering of writing-paper, and carefully placed it in his pocket, then he came to a purple morocco case, which he opened, and there before him, set off by the velvet on which it lay, was the bracelet, a band of dead gold, set with splendid wreaths of forget-me-nots in diamonds and turquoises. George Dallas took it up and examined it attentively, weighed it in his hand, looked closely at the stones in various lights, then replaced it in its case, as a smile of satisfaction spread over his face.

"No mistake about that!" said he. "Even I, all unaccustomed to such luxuries, know that this must be the right thing. She has sent it as she received it, in the very box, with the swell Bond-street jeweller's name and all! Not a bad notion of a present, Mr. Carruthers, by any means. You've money, sir; but, it must be owned, you've taste also. It's only to be hoped that you've not very sharp eyesight, or that you'll ever be tempted to make a very close inspection of the Palais Royal bijouterie which is doing duty for this in the jewel-box! These will set me clear with Routh, and leave me with a few pounds in my pocket besides, to begin life anew with. If it does that, and I can stick to my employment on the *Mercury*, and get a little more work somewhere else, and give up that infernal card-playing—that's the worst of it—I may yet make our friend C. C. believe I am not such a miserable scoundrel as he now imagines me!"

He replaced the case carefully in his breast-pocket, climbed the palings, and was once more on the high road, striding in the direction of Amherst. Ah, the castle-building, only occasionally interrupted by a return to the realities of life in squeezing the packet in his breast-pocket, which he indulged in during that walk! Free, with the chance and the power of making a name for himself in the world! free from all the debasing associations, free from Routh, from Harriet— from Harriet? Was that idea quite so congenial to his feelings? to be separated from Harriet, the only woman whom, in his idle dissipated days, he had ever regarded with anything like affection, the only woman who——and then the bright laughing face and the golden hair of Clare Carruthers rose before his mind. How lovely she was, how graceful and bred-looking, above all, how fresh and youthful, how unsullied by any contact with the world, with all the native instincts pure and original, with no taught captivations or society charms, nothing but—

"Yoho! Yoho!"

George Dallas started from his reverie at the repeated cry, and only just in time sprang from the middle of the road along which, immersed in thought, he had been plodding, as the mail-cart, with its red-faced driver, a sprig of lilac in his breast and a bunch of laburnum behind each ear of his horse, came charging full upon him. The driver was a man, choleric by nature and with a great sense of his position as an important government officer, and he glared round at George and asked him a few rapid questions, in which the devil and his supposed residence were referred to with great volubility. Under less pleasant circumstances Dallas would probably have returned his greeting with interest; as it was, he merely laughed, and, waving his hand, proceeded on his way to the inn, whence, having paid his bill, he returned to London by the first train.

During the whole of the journey up to town the young man's thoughts were filled with his intentions for the future, and no sooner had the train stopped at London-bridge than he determined to go at once to the *Mercury* office and announce his readiness to undertake any amount of work. Accordingly he struck away across the Borough, and, crossing Blackfriars-bridge, dived among a mass of streets running at right angles with Fleet-street, until he arrived at a large, solemn, squat old building, over the door of which glimmered a lamp with the words "Mercury Office" in half-effaced characters. A smart pull

at a sharp, round, big bell brought a preterna-
turally sharp boy to the door, who at once recognised the visitor and admitted him within the
sacred precincts. Up a dark passage, up a steep
and regular flight of stairs, George Dallas proceeded, until on the first floor he rapped at the
door facing him, and, being bidden to come in,
entered the editorial sanctum.

A large cheerless room, its floor covered with
a ragged old Turkey carpet, on its walls two or
three bookshelves crammed with books of reference, two or three maps, an old clock gravely
ticking, and a begrimed bust, with its hair dust-
powdered, and with layers of dust on its highly
developed cheek-bones. In the middle of the
room a battered old desk covered with blue books,
letters opened and unopened, piles of manuscript
under paper-weights, baskets with cards of invitation for all sorts of soirées, entertainments, and
performances, and snake-like india-rubber tubes
for communication with distant printing-offices
or reporters' rooms, a big leaden inkstand like a
bath, and a sheaf of pens more or less dislocated.
At this desk sat a tall man of about fifty, bald-

headed, large-bearded, with sharp gray eyes, well-
cut features, and good presence. This was Mr.
Leigh, editor of the *Mercury;* a man who had
been affiliated to the press from the time of his
leaving college, who had been connected with
nearly all the morning journals in one capacity or
another, correspondent here, manager there, de-
scriptive writer, leader-writer, critic, and scrub,
and who, always rising, had been recommended
by the Jupiter Tonans of the press, the editor of
the *Statesman,* to fill the vacant editorial chair at
the *Mercury.* A long-headed, far-seeing man,
Grafton Leigh, bright as a diamond, and about
as hard, keen as a sword in the hands of a fine
fencer, and as difficult to turn aside, earnest,
energetic, devoted to his work, and caring for
nothing else in comparison—not even for his wife,
then sound asleep in his little house in Brompton,
or his boy working for his exhibition from West-
minster. He looked up as George entered, and
his features, tightly set, relaxed as he recognised
the young man.

"You, Ward!" said he. "We didn't look for
you till to-morrow night. What rush of industry,

what sudden desire to distinguish yourself, has brought you here to-night, my boy?"

Before George could answer, a young man came forward from an inner room, and caught him by the hand.

"What, Paul, old fellow, this is delicious! He must be brimming over with ideas, Chief, and has come down here to ventilate them."

"Not I," said George. "My dear Chief," addressing Leigh, "both you and Cunningham give me credit for more virtue than I possess. I merely looked in as I passed from the railway, to see how things were going on."

"This *is* a sell," said Mr. Cunningham. "I thought I had booked you. You see that confounded Shimmer has failed us again. He was to have done us a sensation leader on the murder—"

"The murder! What murder?"

"O, ah, I forgot; happened since you went away. Wapping or Rotherhithe—some water-side place—body found, and all that kind of thing! Shimmer was to have done us one of his stirrers, full of adjectives, denouncing the supineness of the police, and that kind of thing, and he's never turned up, and the Chief has kept me here to fill his place. Confounded nuisance! I'm obliged to fall back on my old subject—Regulation of the City Traffic!"

"I'm very sorry for you, Cunningham," said George, laughing; "but I can't help you to-night. I'm seedy and tired, and I know nothing about the murder, and want to get to bed. However, I came to tell the Chief that I'm his now and for ever, ready to do double tasks of work from to-morrow out."

"All right, Ward. So long as you don't overdo it, I shall always be delighted to have you with us," said Mr. Leigh. "Now get home to bed, for you look dog-tired." And George Dallas shook hands with each, and went away.

"Glad to hear we're going to have a good deal of work out of Ward, Chief," said Cunningham, when he and his editor were alone again. "He's deuced smart when he likes—as smart as Shimmer, and a great deal more polished and gentlemanly."

"Yes," said Grafton Leigh, "he's a decided catch for the paper. I don't think his health will last, though. Did you notice his manner to-night?—nervous, agitated, and twitching, like a man who had gone through some great excite-ment!"

CHAPTER X.

IT was very late when George Dallas arrived at Routh's lodgings in South Molton-street, so that he felt it necessary to announce his presence by a peculiar knock, known only to the initiated. He made the accustomed signal, but the door was not opened for so abnormally long an interval that he began to think he should have to go away, and defer the telling of the good news until the morning. He had knocked three times, and was about to turn away from the door, when it was noiselessly opened by Harriet herself. She held a shaded candle in her hand, which gave so imperfect a light that Dallas could hardly see her distinctly enough to feel certain that his first impression, that she was looking very pale and ill, was not an imagination induced by the dim light.

She asked him to come into the sitting-room, and said she had just turned the gas out, and was going to bed.

"I am sorry to have disturbed you," he said, when she had set down the candle on a table without re-lighting the gas, "but I want to see Routh particularly. Is he in?"

"No," said Harriet, "he is not. Did you get his letter?"

"What letter? I have not heard from him. I have only just come up from Amherst. But you look ill, Mrs. Routh. Does anything ail you? Is anything wrong?"

"No," she said, hurriedly, "nothing, nothing. Routh has been worried, that's all, and I am very tired."

She pushed the candle further away as she spoke, and, placing her elbow on the table, rested her head on her hand. George looked at her with concern. He had a kind heart and great tenderness for women and children, and he could forget, or, at all events, lay aside his own anxieties in a moment at the sight of suffering in a woman's face. His look of anxious sympathy irritated Harriet; she moved uneasily and impatiently, and said almost harshly:

"Never mind my looks, Mr. Dallas; they don't matter. Tell me how you have sped on your errand at Poynings. Has your mother kept her promise? Have you got the money? I hope so, for I am sorry to say Stewart wants it badly, and has been reckoning on it eagerly. I can't imagine how it happened you did not get his letter."

"I have succeeded," said George. "My mother has kept her word, God bless her, and I came at once to tell Routh he can have the money."

He stopped in the full tide of his animated speech, and looked curiously at Harriet. Something in her manner struck him as being unusual. She was evidently anxious about the money, glad to see him, and yet oddly absent. She did not look at him, and while he spoke she had turned her head sharply once or twice, while her upraised eyelids and parted lips gave her face a fleeting expression of intense listening. She instantly noticed his observation of her, and said sharply:

"Well, pray go on; I am longing to hear your story."

"I thought you were listening to something; you looked as if you heard something," said George.

"So I am listening—to you," Harriet replied, with an attempt at a smile. "So I do hear your adventures. There's nobody up in the house but myself. Pray go on."

So George went on, and told her all that had befallen him at Amherst, with one important reservation; he said nothing of Clare Carruthers or his two meetings with the heiress at the Sycamores; but he told her all about his interview with his mother, and the expedient to which she had resorted to supply his wants. Harriet Routh listened to his story intently; but when she heard that he had received from Mrs. Carruthers, not money, but jewels, she was evidently disconcerted.

"Here is the bracelet," said George, as he took the little packet from the breast-pocket of his coat, and handed it to her. "I don't know much about such things, Mrs. Routh, but perhaps you do. Are the diamonds very valuable?"

Harriet had opened the morocco case containing the bracelet while he was speaking, and now she lifted the beautiful ornament from its satin bed, and held it on her open palm.

"I am not a very capable judge," she said; "but I think these are fine and valuable diamonds. They are extremely beautiful." And a gleam of colour came into her white face as she looked at the gems with a woman's irrepressible admiration of such things.

"I can't tell you how much I feel taking them from her," said George. "It's like a robbery, isn't it?" And he looked full and earnestly at Harriet.

She started, let the bracelet fall, stooped to pick it up, and as she raised her face again, it was whiter than before.

"How can you talk such nonsense?" she said, with a sudden resumption of her usual captivating manner. "Of course it isn't. Do you suppose your mother ever had as much pleasure in these gewgaws in her life as she had in giving them to you? Besides, you know you're going to reform and be steady, and take good advice, are you not?" She watched him very keenly, though her tone was gay and trifling. George reddened, laughed awkwardly, and replied:

"Well, I hope so; and the first step, you know, is to pay my debts. So I must get Routh to put me in the way of selling this bracelet at once. I suppose there's no difficulty about it. I'm sure I have heard it said that diamonds are the same as ready money, and the sooner the tin is in Routh's pocket the better pleased I'll be. None the less obliged to him, though, Mrs. Routh; remember that, both for getting me out of the scrape, and for waiting so long and so good-humouredly for his money."

For all the cordiality of his tone, for all the gratitude he expressed, Harriet felt in her inmost heart, and told herself she felt, that he was a changed man; that he felt his freedom, rejoiced in it, and did not mean again to relinquish or endanger it.

"The thing he feared has happened," she thought, while her small white fingers were busy with the jewels. "The very thing he feared. This man must be got away—how am I to do it?"

The solitary candle was burning dimly; the room was dull, cold, and gloomy. George looked round, and was apparently thinking of taking his leave, when Harriet said:

"I have not told you how opportune your getting this money—for I count it as money— is. Stay; let me light the gas. Sit down there opposite to me, and you shall hear how things have gone with us since you went away." She had thrown off the abstraction of her manner, and in a moment she lighted the gas, put the extinguished candle out of sight, set wine upon the table, and pulled a comfortable arm-chair forward, in which she begged George to seat himself. "Take off your coat," she said; and he obeyed her, telling her, with a laugh, as he flung it upon a chair, that there was a small parcel of soiled linen in the pocket.

"I did not expect to have to stay at Amherst, so I took no clothes with me," he explained, "and had to buy a shirt and a pair of stockings for Sunday, so as not to scandalise the natives. Rather an odd place to replenish one's wardrobe, by the bye."

Harriet looked sharply at the coat, and, passing the chair on which it lay on her way to her
own, felt its texture with a furtive touch. Then
she sat down, gave Dallas wine, and once more
fell to examining the bracelet. It might have
occurred to any other man in George's position
that it was rather an odd proceeding on the
part of Mrs. Routh to keep him there at so late
an hour with no apparent purpose, and without
any expressed expectation of Routh's return; but
George seldom troubled himself with reflections
upon anybody's conduct, and invariably followed
Harriet's lead without thinking about it at all.
Recent events had shaken Routh's influence, and
changed the young man's views and tastes, but
Harriet still occupied her former place in his
regard and in his habit of life, which in such
cases as his signifies much. With a confidential
air she now talked to him, her busy fingers twist-
ing the bracelet as she spoke, her pale face turned
to him, but her eyes somewhat averted. She
told him that Routh had been surprised and annoyed at his (Dallas) being so long away from
town, and had written to him, to tell him that

he had been so pressed for money, so worried by duns, and so hampered by the slow proceedings of the company connected with the new speculation, that he had been obliged to go away, and must keep away, until Dallas could let him have one hundred and forty pounds. George was concerned to hear all this, and found it hard to reconcile with the good spirits in which Routh had been when he had seen him last; but he really knew so little of the man's affairs beyond having a general notion that they were hopelessly complicated, and subject to volcanic action of an utterly disconcerting nature, that he regarded his own surprise as unreasonable, and forbore to express it.

"It is of the utmost importance to Stewart to have the money at once," Harriet continued. "You see that, yourself; he told you all in his letter."

"Very extraordinary it should have been lost! Directed to P. O., Amherst, of course? I wish I had got it, Mrs. Routh; I'd have gone at once and sold the bracelet before I came to you at all, and brought the money. But I can do it early in the morning, can't I? I can take it to

some good jeweller and get cash for it, and be
here by twelve o'clock, so as not to keep Routh
a moment longer than I need in suspense. Will
a hundred and forty square him for the present,
Mrs. Routh? I'm sure to get more for the bracelet—don't you think so?—and of course he can
have it all, if he wants it."

The young man spoke in an eager tone, and
the woman listened with a swelling heart. Her
full red lip trembled for a passing instant—consideration for—kindness to the only human creature she loved touched Harriet as nothing besides
had power to touch her.

"I am sure the bracelet is worth more than
that sum," she said; "it is worth more than
two hundred pounds, I dare say. But you forget,
Mr. Dallas, that you must not be too precipitate
in this matter. It is of immense importance to
Stewart to have this money, but there are precautions to be taken."

"Precautions, Mrs. Routh! what precautions?
The bracelet's my own, isn't it, and principally
valuable because there's no bother about selling
a thing of the kind?"

She looked at him keenly; she was calculating to what extent she might manage him, how far he would implicitly believe her statements, and rely upon her judgment. His countenance was eminently reassuring, so she went on :

"Certainly the bracelet is your own, and it could be easily sold, were you only to consider yourself, but you have your mother to consider."

"My mother! How? when she has parted with the bracelet on purpose."

"True," said Harriet; "but perhaps you are not aware that diamonds, of anything like the value of these, are as well known, their owners, buyers, and whereabouts, as blood horses, their pedigrees, and purchasers. I think it would be unsafe for you to sell this bracelet in London; you may be sure the diamonds would be known by any jeweller on whose respectability you could sufficiently rely, to sell the jewels to him. It would be very unpleasant, and of course very dangerous to your mother, if the diamonds were known to be those purchased by Mr. Carruthers, and a cautious jeweller thought proper to ask him any questions."

George looked grave and troubled, as Harriet put these objections to his doing as he had proposed, for the immediate relief of Routh, clearly before him. He never for a moment doubted the accuracy of her information, and the soundness of her fears.

"I understand," he said; "but what can I do? I must sell the bracelet to get the money, and sooner or later will make no difference in the risk you speak of; but it may make all the difference to Routh. I can't, I won't delay in this matter; don't ask me, Mrs. Routh. It is very generous of you to think of my risk, but—"

"It is not your risk," she interrupted him by saying; "it is your mother's. If it were your own, I might let you take it, for Stewart's sake" —an indefinable compassion was in the woman's face, an unwonted softness in her blue eyes— "but your mother has done and suffered much for you, and she must be protected, even if Stewart has to lie hidden a day or two longer. You must not do anything rash. I think I know what would be the best thing for you to do."

"Tell me, Mrs. Routh," said George, who

highly appreciated the delicate consideration for his mother which inspired Harriet's misgivings. "Tell me, and whatever it is, I will do it."

"It is this," said Harriet; "I know there is a large trade in diamonds at Amsterdam, and that the merchants there, chiefly Jews, deal in the loose stones, and are not, in our sense, jewellers. You could dispose of the diamonds there without suspicion or difficulty; it is the common resort of people who have diamonds to sell—London is not. If you would go there at once, you might sell the diamonds, and send the money to Stewart, or rather to me, to an address we would decide upon, without more than the delay of a couple of days. Is there anything to keep you in town?"

"No," said George, "nothing. I could start this minute, as far as any business I've got to do is concerned."

Harriet drew a long breath, and her colour rose.

"I wish you would, Mr. Dallas," she said, earnestly. "I hardly like to urge you, it seems so selfish; and Stewart, if he were here, would make so much lighter of the difficulty he is in than I can bring myself to do, but you don't know how grateful I should be to you if you would."

The pleading earnestness of her tone, the eager entreaty in her eyes, impressed George painfully; he hastened to assure her that he would accede to any request of hers.

"I am so wretched when he is away from me, Mr. Dallas," said Harriet; "I am so lonely and full of dread. Anything not involving you or your mother in risk, which would shorten the time of his absence, would be an unspeakable boon to me."

"Then of course I will go at once, Mrs. Routh," said George. "I will go to-morrow. I am sure you are quite right, and Amsterdam's the place to do the trick at. I wish I could have seen Routh first, for a moment, but as I can't, I can't. Let me see. Amsterdam. There's a boat to Rotterdam by the river, and—O, by Jove! here's a Bradshaw; let's see when the next goes."

He walked to the little sideboard, and selected the above-named compendium of useful knowledge from a mass of periodicals, circulars, bills, and prospectuses of companies immediately to be brought out, and offering unheard-of advantages to the investors.

The moment his eyes were turned away from her, a fierce impatience betrayed itself in Harriet's face, and as he sat slowly turning over the sibylline leaves, and consulting the incomprehensible and maddening index, she pressed her clasped hands against her knees, as though it were almost impossible to resist the impulse which prompted her to tear the book from his dilatory fingers.

"Here it is," said George, at length, "and uncommonly cheap, too. The Argus for Rotterdam, seven A.M. That's rather early, though, isn't it? To-morrow morning, too, or rather this morning, for it's close upon one now. Let's see when the Argus, or some other boat, goes next. H'm; not till Thursday at the same hour. That's rather far off."

Harriet was breathing quickly, and her face was quite white, but she sat still and controlled her agony of anxiety. "I have urged him as strongly as I dare," she thought; "fate must do the rest."

Fate did the rest.

"After all, I may as well go at seven in the morning, Mrs. Routh. All my things are packed up already, and it will give me a good start. I might get my business done before Wednesday night, almost, if I'm quick about it; at all events early the following day."

" You might, indeed," said Harriet, in a faint voice.

"There's one little drawback, though, to that scheme," said Dallas. "I haven't the money. They owe me a trifle at the *Mercury*, and I shall have to wait till to-morrow and get it, and go by Ostend, the swell route. I can't go without it, that's clear."

Harriet looked at him with a wan blank face, in which there was something of weariness, and under it something of menace, but her tone was quite amiable and obliging as she said:

" I think it is a pity to incur botli delay and expense by waiting. I have always a little ready money by me, in case of our having to make a move suddenly, or of an illness, or one of the many contingencies which men never think of, and women never forget. You can have it with pleasure. You can return it to me," she said, with a forced smile, "when you send Routh the hundred and forty."

"Thank you," said Dallas. "I shan't mind taking it from you for a day or two, as it is to send help to Routh the sooner. Then I'll go, that's settled, and I had better leave you, for you were tired when I came in, and you must be still more tired now. I shall get back from Amsterdam as quickly as I can, tell Routh, but I see my way to making a few pounds out of the place. They want padding at the *Mercury*, and I shan't come back by return of post." He had risen now, and had extended his hand towards the bracelet, which lay in its open case on the table.

A sudden thought struck Harriet.

"Stop," she said; "I don't think it would do to offer this bracelet in its present shape, any-where. The form and the setting are too remark-able. It would probably be re-sold entire, and it is impossible to say what harm might come of its being recognised. It must be taken to pieces, and you must offer the diamonds separately for sale. It will make no appreciable difference in the money you will receive, for such work as this is like bookbinding — dear to buy, but never counted in the price when you want to sell."

" What am I to do, then?" asked George, in a dismayed tone. "I could not to take out the diamonds, you know; they are firmly set—see here." He turned the gold band inside out, and showed her the plain flat surface at the back of the diamonds and turquoises.

" Wait a moment," said Harriet. "I think I can assist you in this respect. Do you study the bracelet a bit until I come to you."

She left the room, and remained away for a little time. Dallas stood close by the table, having lowered the gas-burners, and by their light he closely inspected the rivets, the fastenings, and the general form of the splendid ornament he was so anxious to get rid of, idly thinking how well it must have looked on his mother's still beautiful arm, and wondering whether she was likely soon to be obliged to wear the counterfeit. His back was turned to the door by which Harriet had left the room, so that, when she came softly to the aperture again, he did not perceive her. She carefully noted his attitude, and glided softly in, carrying several small implements in her right hand, and in her left held cautiously behind her back a coat, which she dexterously dropped upon the floor quite unperceived by Dallas, behind the chair on which he had thrown his. She then went up to the table, and showed him a small pair of nippers, a pair of scissors of peculiar form, and a little implement, with which she told him workers in jewelry loosened stones in their setting, and punched them out. Dallas looked with some surprise at the collection, regarding them as unusual items of a lady's paraphernalia, and said, gaily :

"You are truly a woman of resources, Mrs. Routh. Who would ever have thought of your having all those things ready at a moment's notice?"

Harriet made no reply, but she could not quite conceal the disconcerting effect of his words.

"If I have made a blunder in this," she thought, "it is a serious one, but I have more to do, and must not think yet."

She sat down, cleared a space on the table, placed the bracelet and the little tools before her, and set to work at once at her task of demolition. It was a long one, and the sight was pitiful as, she placed jewel after jewel carefully in a small box before her, and proceeded to loosen one after another. Sometimes George took the bracelet from her and aided her, but the greater part of the work was done by her. The face bent over the disfigured gold and maltreated gems was a remarkable one in its mingled expression of intentness and absence; her will was animating her fingers in their task, but her mind, her fancy, her memory, were away, and, to judge by the rigidity of the cheeks and lips, the unrelaxed tension of the low white brow, on no pleasing excursion. The pair worked on in silence, only broken occasionally by a word from George, expressive of admiration for her dexterity and the celerity with which she detached the jewels from the gold setting. At length all was done—the golden band, limp and scratched, was a mere commonplace piece of goldsmith's work—the diamonds lay in their box in a shining heap, the discarded turquoises on the table; and all was done.

"What shall we do with these things?" asked George. "They are not worth selling—at least, not now—but I think the blue things might make up prettily with the gold again. Will you keep them, Mrs. Routh? and some day, when I am better off, I'll have them set for you, in re-membrance of this night in particular, and of all your goodness to me in general."

He was looking at the broken gold and the turquoises, thinking how trumpery they looked now—not at her. Fortunately not at her, for if he had seen her face he must have known—even he, unsuspicious as he was—that she was shaken by some inexplicably powerful feeling. The dark blood rushed into her face, dispersed itself over her fair throat in blotches, and made a sudden dreadful tingling in her ears. For a minute she did not reply, and then Dallas did look at her, but the agony had passed over her.

"No—no," she said; "the gold is valuable, and the turquoises as much so as they can be for their size. You must keep them for a rainy day."

"I'm likely to see many," said George, with half a smile and half a sigh, "but I don't think I'll ever use these things to keep me from the pelting of the pitiless shower. If you won't keep them for yourself, Mrs. Routh, perhaps you'll keep them for me until I return."

"O, yes," said Harriet, "I will keep them. I will lock them up in my desk; you will know where to find them."

She drew the desk towards her as she spoke, took out of it a piece of paper, without seeing that one side had some writing upon it, swept the scattered turquoises into the sheet, then folded the gold band in a second, placed both in a large blue envelope, with the device of Routh's last new company scheme upon it, and sealed the parcel over the wafer.

"Write your name on it," she said to George, who took up a pen and obeyed her. She opened a drawer at the side of the desk, and put away the little parcel quite at the back. Then she took from the same drawer seven sovereigns, which George said would be as much as he would require for the present, and which he carefully stowed away in his pocket-book. Then he sat down at the desk, and playfully wrote an I O U for the amount.

"That's business-like," said George, smiling, but the smile by which she replied was so wan and weary, that George again commented on her fatigue, and began to take leave of her.

"I'm off, then," he said, "and you won't forget to tell Routh how much I wanted to see him. Among other things to tell him— However, I suppose he has seen Deane since I have been away?"

Harriet was occupied in turning down the gas-burner by which she had just lighted the candle again. She now said:

"How stupid I am! as if 1 couldn't have lighted you to the door first, and put the gas out afterwards! The truth is, I am so tired; I'm quite stupefied. What did you say, Mr. Dallas? There, I've knocked your coat off the chair; here it is, however. You asked me something, I think?"

George took the coat she held from her, hung it over his arm, felt for his hat (the room being lighted only by the feeble candle), and repeated his words:

"Routh has seen Deane, of course, since I've been away?"

"No," Harriet replied with distinctness, "he has not—he has not."

"Indeed!" said George. "I am surprised at that. But Deane was huffed, I remember, on Tuesday, when Routh broke his engagement to dine with him, and said it must depend on whether he was in the humour to meet him the next day, as Routh asked him to do. So I suppose he wasn't in the humour, eh? And now he'll be huffed with me, but I can't help it."

"Why?" asked Harriet; and she spoke the single word with a strange effort, and a painful dryness of the throat.

"Because I promised to give him his revenge at billiards. I won ten pounds from him that night, and uncommonly lucky it was for me; it enabled me to get away from my horrible old shrew of a landlady, and, indeed, indirectly it enables me to start on this business to-morrow."

"How?" said Harriet. Again she spoke but

one word, and again with difficulty and a dryness in the throat. She set down the candle, and leaned against the table, while George stood between her and the door, his coat over his arm.

"You didn't notice that I told you I was all packed up and ready to go. It happened, luckily, didn't it?" And then George told his listener how he had paid his landlady, and removed his modest belongings on the previous Wednesday morning to a coffee-house, close to the river too. "By Jove! I'm in luck's way, it seems," he said; "so I shall merely go and sleep there, and take my traps on board the Argus. I have only such clothes as I shall want, no matter where I am," he said. "They'll keep the trunk with my books until I come back, and Deane must wait for his revenge with the balls and cues for the same auspicious occasion. Let's hope he'll be in a better temper, and have forgiven Routh. He was awfully riled at his note on Tuesday evening."

"Did—did you see it?" asked Harriet; and, as she spoke, she leaned still more heavily against the table.

"No," replied Dallas, "I did not; but Deane

told me Routh asked him to meet him the next day. He didn't, it seems."

"No," said Harriet; "and Stewart is very much annoyed about it. Mr. Deane owed him money, and he asked him for some in that note."

"Indeed," said George; "he could have paid him then. I happen to know. He had a lot of gold and notes with him. The tenner he lost to me he paid in a note, and he changed a fiver to pay for our dinner, and he was bragging and bouncing the whole time about the money he had about him, and what he would, and would not, do with it. So it was sheer spite made him neglect to pay Routh, and I hope he'll dun him again. The idea of Routh being in the hole he's in, and a fellow like that owing him money. How much is it, Mrs. Routh?"

"I—I don't know," said Harriet.

"There, I'm keeping you talking still. I am the most thoughtless fellow." It never occurred to George that she had kept him until she had learned what she wanted to know. "Good-bye, Mrs. Routh, good-bye."

She had passed him, the candle in her hand,

and this farewell was uttered in the hall. He held out his hand; she hesitated for a moment, and then gave him hers. He pressed it fervently; it was deadly cold.

"Don't stay in the chill air," he said; "you are shivering now."

Then he went away with a light cheerful step.

Harriet Routh stood quite still, as he had left her, for one full minute; then she hurried into the sitting-room, shut the door, dropped on her knees before a chair, and ground her face fiercely against her arms. There she knelt, not sobbing, not weeping, but shuddering—shuddering with the quick terrible iteration of mortal agony of spirit, acting on an exhausted frame. After a while she rose, and then her face was dreadful to look upon, in its white fixed despair.

"If I have saved him," she said, as she sat wearily down by the table again, and once more leaned her face upon her hands—"if I have saved him! It may be there is a chance; at all events, there is a chance. How wonderful, how inconceivably wonderful that he should not have heard of it! The very stones of the street seem to cry it out, and he has not heard of it; the very air is full of it, and he knows nothing. If any thing should prevent his going? But no; nothing will, nothing *can*. This was the awful danger—this was the certain, the inevitable risk; if I have averted it; if I have saved him, for the time!"

The chill of coming dawn struck cold to her limbs, the sickness of long watching, of fear, and of sleeplessness was at her heart, but Harriet Routh did not lie down on her bed all that dreadful night. Terrible fatigue weighed down her eyelids, and made her flesh tremble and quiver over the aching bones.

"I must not sleep—I should not wake in time," she said, as she forced herself to rise from her chair, and paced the narrow room, when the sudden numbness of sleep threatened to fall upon her. "I have something to do."

Dawn came, then sunrise, then the sounds, the stir of morning. Then Harriet bathed her face in cold water, and looked in her toilet-glass at her haggard features. The image was not re-assuring; but she only smiled a bitter smile, and made a mocking gesture with her hand.

"Never any more," she murmured—"never any more.'

The morning was cold and raw, but Harriet heeded it not. She glanced out of the window of her bedroom before she left it, wearing her bonnet and shawl, and closely veiled. Then she closed the shutters, locked the door, withdrew the key, and came into the sitting-room. She went to a chair and took up a coat which lay at the back of it; then she looked round for a moment as if in search of something. Her eye lighted on a small but heavy square of black marble which lay on the writing-table, and served as a paper-press. She then spread the coat on the table, placed the square of marble on it, and rolled it tightly round the heavy centre, folding and pressing the parcel into the smallest possible dimensions. This done, she tied it tightly with a strong cord, and, concealing it under her shawl, went swiftly out of the house. No one saw her issue from the grim, gloomy door—the neighbouring housemaids had not commenced their matutinal task of door-step cleaning, alleviated by gossip— and she went away down the street, completely unobserved. Went away, with her head down, her face hidden, with a quick, steady step and an unfaltering purpose. There were not many wayfarers abroad in the street, and of those she saw none, and was remarked by only one.

Harriet Routh took her way towards the river, and reached Westminster-bridge as the clock in the great tower of the new palace marked half-past six. All was quiet. A few of the laggards of the working classes were straggling across the bridge to their daily toil, a few barges were moving sluggishly upon the muddy water; but there was no stir, no business yet. Harriet lingered when she had reached the centre of the bridge; a figure was just vanishing at the southern end, the northern was clear of people. She leaned over the parapet, and looked down—no boat, no barge was near. Then she dropped the parcel she had carried into the river, and the water closed over it. Without the delay of an instant, she turned and retraced her steps towards home. As she neared South Molton-street, she found several of the shops open, and entering one, she purchased a black marble letter-press.

It was not precisely similar to that with which she had weighted the parcel, which now lay in the bed of the river; but the difference was trifling, and not to be perceived by the eye of a stranger.

Near the house in which the Rouths occupied apartments there was an archway which formed the entrance to some mews. As she passed this open space, Harriet's glance fell upon the inquisitive countenance of a keen-looking, ragged street-boy, who was lying contentedly on his back under the archway, with his arms under his head, and propped upon the kerbstone. A sudden impulse arrested her steps. "Have you no other place to lie than here?" she asked the boy, who jumped up with great alacrity, and stood before her in an attitude almost respectful.

"Yes, ma'am," he said, "I have, but I'm here, waiting for an early job."

She gave him a shilling and a smile—not such a smile as she once had to give, but the best that was left her—and went on to the door of the house she lived in. She opened it with a key, and went in.

The boy remained where she had left him,

apparently ruminating, and wagging his tousled head sagely.

" Whatever is *she* up to ?" he asked of himself, in perplexity. " It's a rum start, as far as I knows on it, and I means to know more. But how is *she* in it ? I shan't say nothing till I knows more about that." And then Mr. Jim Swain went his way to a more likely quarter for early jobs.

Fortune favoured Mrs. Routh on that morning. She gained her bedroom unseen and unheard, and having hastily undressed, lay down to rest, if rest would come to her—at least to await in quiet the ordinary hour at which the servant was accustomed to call her. It came, and passed; but Harriet did not rise.

She slept a little when all the world was up and busy—slept until the second delivery of letters brought one for her, which the servant took at once to her room.

The letter was from George Dallas, and contained merely a few lines, written when he was on the point of starting, and posted at the riverside. He apologised to Harriet for a mistake which he had made on the previous night. He had taken up Routh's coat instead of his own, and had not discovered the error until he was on his way to the steamer, and it was too late to repair it. He hoped it would not matter, as he had left his own coat at South Molton-street, and no doubt Routh could wear it, on an occasion.

When Harriet had read this note, she lay back upon her pillow, and fell into a deep sleep which was broken by Routh's coming into her room early in the afternoon. He looked pale and haggard, and he stood by the bedside in silence. But she —she sat up, and flung her arms round him with a wonderfully good imitation of her former manner; and when she told him all that had passed, her husband caught her to his breast with passionate fondness and gratitude, and declared over and over again that her ready wit and wonderful fortitude had saved him.

Saved him? How, and from what?

CHAPTER XI.

LIFE at Poynings had its parallel in hundreds of of country-houses, of which it was but a type. It was a life essentially English in its character, in its staid respectability, in its dull decorum. There are old French chateaux without number, visible in bygone days to travellers in the banquettes of diligences, and glimpses of which may still occasionally be caught from the railways, gray, square, four pepper-box turreted old buildings, wherein life is dreary but not decorous, and sad without being staid. It is the day-dream of many an English country gentleman that his house should, in the first place, be respectable, in the second place, comfortable, in the third place, free from damp; after these successes are achieved, he takes no further thought for it; within and without the dulness may be soul-harrowing; that is no affair of his. So long as his dining-room is large enough to contain the four-and-twenty guests who, on selected moonlight nights, are four times in every year bidden to share his hospitality—so long as the important seignorial dignities derivable from the possession of lodge, and stable, and kennel are maintained—so long as the state devolving upon him as justice of the peace, with a scarcely defined hope of one day arriving at the position of deputy-lieutenant, is kept up, vaulting ambition keeps itself within bounds, and the young English country gentleman is satisfied.

More than satisfied, indeed, was Mr. Capel Carruthers in the belief that all the requirements above named were properly fulfilled. In his earlier life he had been haunted by a dim conviction that he was rather an ass than otherwise; he remembered that that had been the verdict returned at Rugby, and his reflections on his very short career at Cambridge gave him no reason to doubt the decision of his schoolfellows. Not a pleasant source of reflection even to a man of Mr. Carruthers's blunted feelings; in fact, a depressing, wrong, Radical state of mind, for which there was only

one antidote—the thought that he was Mr. Carruthers of Poynings, a certain settled stable posi-
sition which would have floated its possessor over
any amount of imbecility. Carruthers of Poynings! There it was in old county histories, with
a genealogy of the family and a charming copper
engraving of Poynings at the beginning of the
century, with two ladies in powder and hoops
fishing in an impossible pond, and a gentleman
in a cocked-hat and knee-breeches pointing out
nothing in particular to nobody at all. Carruthers
of Poynings! All the old armour in the hall,
hauberks and breastplates, now propped upon a
slight wooden frame, instead of enclosing the big
chests and the thews and sinews which they had
preserved through the contests of the rival Roses
or the Cavaliers and Roundheads—all the old
ancestors hanging round the dining-room, soldiers,
courtiers, Kentish yeomen, staring with grave
eyes at the smug white-whiskered old gentleman,
their descendant—all the old tapestry worked by
Maud Carruthers, whose husband was killed in
the service of Mary Stuart—all the carvings and
gildings about the house, all the stained glass in

the windows, all the arms and quartering and
crests upon the family plate—all whispered to the
present representative of the family that he was
Carruthers of Poynings, and as such had only to
make a very small effort to find life no very difficult matter, even for a person scantily endowed
with brains. He tried it accordingly—tried it
when a young man, had pursued the course ever
since, and found it successful. Any latent suspicion of his own want of wisdom had vanished
long since, as how, indeed, could it last? When
Mr. Carruthers took his seat as chairman of the
magisterial bench at Amherst, he found himself
listening with great admiration to the prefatory
remarks which he addressed to the delinquent in
custody before passing sentence on him, unconscious that those remarks only echoed the magistrate's clerk, who stood close behind him whis-
pering into his ear. When, as was his regular
custom, he walked round the barn, where, on rent-
days, the tenants were assembled at dinner, and
heard his health proposed in glowing terms, and
drunk with great enthusiasm—for he was a good
and liberal landlord—and when he addressed a

few conventional words of thanks in reply, and
stroked his white whiskers, and bowed, amidst
renewed cheering, how should a thought of his
own shortcomings ever dawn upon him?

His shortcomings!—the shortcomings of Mr.
Carruthers of Poynings? If, indeed, in his earlier
days there had been a latent belief in the existence of anything so undesirable and so averse
to the proper status of a county magnate, it had
long since died out. It would have been hard and
unnatural, indeed, for a man so universally re-
spected and looked up to, not to give in to the
general creed, and admit that there were un-
doubted grounds for the wide-spread respect
which he enjoyed.   There are two kinds of
"squires," to use the old English word, who exercise equal influence on the agricultural mind,
though in very different ways. The one is the
type which Fielding loved to draw, and which has
very little altered since his time—the jocund
sporting man, rib-poking, lass-chin-chucking
franklin, the tankard-loving, cross-country-riding,
oath-using, broad-skirted, cord-breeched, white-
hatted squire.   The other is the landed pro-

prietor, magistrate, patron of the living, chairman of the board of guardians, supporter of the
church and state, pattern man. Mr. Carruthers of Poynings belonged to the latter class.
You could have told that by a glance at him on
his first appearance in the morning, with his chin
shaved clean, his well-brushed hair and whiskers,
his scrupulously white linen, his carefully tied
check neckcloth, his portentous collars, his trim-
med and polished nails. His very boots creaked
of position and respectability, and his large white
waistcoat represented unspotted virtue. Looking
at him ensconced behind the bright-edged Bible at
early morning prayers, the servants believed in
the advantages derivable from a correct life, and
made an exception in their master's favour to the
doom of Dives. By his own measure he meted
the doings of others, and invariably arose considerably self-refreshed from the mensuration.
Hodge, ploughman, consigned to the cage after a
brawl with Giles, hedger, consequent upon a too
liberal consumption of flat and muddy ale at The
Three Horseshoes, known generally as The Shoes,
and brought up for judgment before the bench,

pleading " a moog too much" in extenuation, might count on scanty commiseration from the magistrate, who never exceeded his four glasses of remarkably sound claret. Levi Hinde, gipsy and tramp, arraigned for stealing a loaf from a baker's shop—as he said, to save the life of his starving child—impressed not one whit the portly chairman of the Amherst branch of the County Bank. Mr. Carruthers never got drunk, and never committed theft; and that there could be any possible temptation for other people so to act, was beyond the grasp of his most respectable imagination.

A man of his stamp generally shows to the least advantage in his domestic relations. Worshipped from a distance by outsiders, who, when occasion forces them into the presence, approach, metaphorically, in the Siamese fashion, on hands and knees, there is usually a good deal too much Grand Lama-like mystery and dignity about the recipient of all this homage to render him agreeable to those with whom he is brought into daily contact. Mr. Carruthers was not an exception to the rule. He had a notion that love, except the extremely respectable but rather weak regard felt by mothers towards their infants, was a ridiculous boy-and-girl sentiment, which never really came to anything, nor could be considered worthy of notice until the feminine mind was imbued with a certain amount of reverence for the object of her affection. Mr. Carruthers had never read Tennyson (in common with his class, he was extremely severe upon poets in general, looking upon them not merely as fools, but as idle mischievous fools, who might be better employed in earning a decent livelihood, say as carters or turnpike-men); but he was thoroughly impressed with the idea that "woman is the lesser man," and he felt that any open display of affection on his part towards his wife might militate against what he considered entirely essential to his domestic happiness—his "being looked up to." He was in the habit of treating his wife in ordinary matters of social intercourse very much as he treated the newly-appointed justice of the peace at the meetings of the magisterial bench, viz. as a person whose position was now recognised by the laws of society as equal to their own, but who must nevertheless feel inwardly that between him and Mr.

Carruthers of Poynings there was really a great gulf fixed, the bridging of which, however easy it may appear, was really a matter of impossibility.

If these feelings existed, as they undoubtedly did in Mr. Carruthers under the actual circumstances of his marriage, it may be imagined that they would have been much keener, much more intensified, had he taken to wife, instead of the quiet widow lady whom, to the astonishment of the county, he chose, any of the dashing girls who had danced, dressed, and flirted at him perseveringly, but in vain. Poynings was a sufficiently nice place to render its master a catch in the county, and to induce husband-hunting misses to discount his age and pomposity, so that when the cards of Mr. and Mr. Capel Carruthers were sent round (it was before the contemptuous days of "no cards"), and it was discovered that the new mistress of Poynings was somebody quite out of "the set," immediately "that dear Mr. Carruthers" became "that horrid old thing," and it required years of open-handed hospitality to reëstablish him in favour.

But Capel Carruthers had chosen wisely, and

he knew it. With all his weakness and vanity, a
gentleman in thought and tastes, he had taken for
his wife a lady whose birth and breeding must
have been acknowledged in any society; a lady
whose age was not ill-suited to his own, whose
character was unimpeachable, who was thoroughly
qualified to superintend the bringing out of his
niece, and whose sole vulnerable point for criticism
—her poverty—was rendered invulnerable as soon
as she became Mrs. Carruthers of Poynings. And,
under all the cold placid exterior which never
thawed, under all the set Grandisonian forms of
speech which were never relaxed, under the judicial
manner and the Board-of-Guardians address, flowed
a warm current of love for his wife which he himself scarcely suspected. With such poor brains as
he had, he had occasionally fallen to the task of
self-examination, asking himself how it was that
he, Mr. Carruthers of Poynings (even in his
thoughts he liked the ring of that phrase), could
have so far permitted himself to be swayed by
any one, and then he told himself that he was
reverenced and looked up to, that his state, position, and dignities were duly acknowledged, and

in a satisfied frame of mind he closed the self-colloquy. Loved his wife—eh! neither he nor any one else knew how much. George Dallas need not have been anxious about the treatment of his mother by his step-father. When the young man cursed his exile from his mother's presence and his step-father's home, he little knew the actual motives which prompted Mr. Carruthers to decide upon and to keep rigidly in force that decree of banishment. Not only his step-son's wildness and extravagance; though a purist, Mr. Carruthers was sufficient man of the world to know that in most cases there are errors of youth which correct themselves in the flight of time. Not a lurking fear that his niece, thrown in this prodigal's way, should be dazzled by the glare of his specious gifts, and singe her youth and innocence in their baleful light. Not a dread of having to notice and recognise the young man as his connection in the chastened arena of county society.

As nature had not endowed Mr. Carruthers with a capacity for winning affection, though it was not to be denied that there were qualities in his character which commanded respect, it was fortunate for him that he cared less about the former than the latter. Nevertheless, he would probably have been rendered very uncomfortable, not to say unhappy, had he supposed that his wife, "Mrs. Carruthers of Poynings," as there is reason to suppose he designated her, even in his inmost thoughts, positively did not love him. Such a supposition, however, never had occurred to him, which was fortunate; for Mr. Carruthers was apt to hold by his suppositions as strongly as other people held by their convictions, as, indeed, being *his*, why should he not? and it would have been very difficult to dislodge such a notion. The notion itself would have been, in the first place, untrue, and in the second dangerous. Mrs. Carruthers of Poynings loved her rather grim and decidedly uninteresting but unimpeachably respectable husband, if not passionately, which was hardly to be expected, very sincerely, and estimated him after the fashion of wives—that is to say, considerably above his deserts. All women like their husbands, except those who notoriously do not, and Mrs. Carruthers was no exception to the rule. She had a much greater sense of jus-

tice in her than most women, and she used it
practically—applied it to her own case. She knew
the fault had been her son's in the great sorrow
which had destroyed all the pride and pleasure
which her prosperous marriage would otherwise
have brought her, and she did not charge it upon
her husband, or, except in so far as her uncon-
querable anxiety and depression caused him annoyance, did she inflict the penalty of it on him.
She knew him to be a hard man, and she did not
look for softness from him; but she accepted
such advantages as hardness of character possesses,
and bore its disadvantages well. "If I were he,"
she had said to herself, even in the first hours of
her anguish of conviction of her boy's unworthiness, and when his step-father's edict of exclusion
was but newly published, "and I had so little
knowledge of human nature as he has, if life had
never taught me toleration, if Clare were my
niece and George his son, would I not have acted
as he has done? He is consistent to the justness
and the sternness of his character." Thinking
thus, Mrs. Carruthers acted on the maxim that
to judge others aright we should put ourselves in

their position. So she accepted the great trial of
her life, and suffered it as quietly and patiently
as she could. It would be difficult to define with
precision the nature of Mr. Carruthers's senti-
ments towards George Dallas. The young man
had met his step-father but rarely, and had on
each occasion increased the disfavour with which
from the first the elder man had regarded him.
He had never tried to propitiate, had, indeed,
regarded him with contemptuous indifference,
secure in what he fancied to be the security of
his mother's position; and there had been covert
antagonism between them from the first. How
much astonished Mr. Carruthers would have been
had any revelation been made to him of the
secrets of his own heart, whereby he would have
discovered that a strong sentiment of jealousy lay
at the root of his antipathy to George Dallas —
jealousy which intensified his hardness and sternness, and forbade him to listen to the promptings
of common sense, which told him that the line he
was taking towards the son was so cruel to the
mother as to neutralise all the advantages presented by the fine marriage she had made, and

for which, by the way, he expected her to
be constantly demonstratively grateful. In this
expectation he was as constantly disappointed.
Mrs. Carruthers was an eminently *true* woman,
and as she felt no peculiar exuberance of gratitude, she showed none. She was a lady too—
much more perfectly a lady than Mr. Carruthers
was unimpeachably a gentleman—and, as such,
she filled her position as a matter of course, as
she would have filled one much higher, or one
much lower, and thought nothing about it. She
was of so much finer a texture, so much higher a
nature than her husband, that she did not suspect him of any double motive in his treatment
of George Dallas. She never dreamed that Mr.
Carruthers of Poynings was secretly uneasily
jealous of the man who had died in his prime
many years before, and the son, who had been
first the young widow's sole consolation and then
her bitterest trial. The living and the dead combined to displease Mr. Carruthers, and he would
have been unequivocally glad, only in decorous
secrecy, could he have obtained any evidence to
prove that George Dallas was remarkably like his

father in all the defective points of his personal
appearance and in all the faults of his character.
But such evidence was not within his reach, and
Mr. Carruthers was reduced to hoping in his
secret heart that his suppositions were correct on
this point, and discovering a confirmation of them
in his wife's scrupulous silence with regard to
her first husband. She had never, in their most
confidential moments, remarked on any likeness
between George and his father; had never, indeed, mentioned Captain Dallas at all, which
appeared extremely significant to Mr. Carruthers,
but seeing that Captain Dallas had been dead
twelve years when his widow became Mrs. Carruthers of Poynings, would not have occasioned
much surprise to the world in general. Mr. Carruthers regarded himself as his wife's benefactor,
but she did not partake of his views in that respect. The notion which he entertained of his
position with regard to his niece Clare was better
founded and more reasonable.

The beautiful young heiress, who was an unconscious and involuntary element in the standing
grievance of Mrs. Carruthers's life, was the only

child of Mr. Carruthers's brother, and the sole inheritor of his property. Her father had died while she was a little child, and her mother's method of educating her has been already described. She was attached to her uncle, but was afraid of him; and she was happier and more at ease at the Sycamores than at Poynings. Of course Mr. Carruthers did not suspect his niece of any such depravity of taste. It never occurred to him that any one could fancy himself or herself happier anywhere on the face of the created globe than at Poynings; and so Clare escaped the condemnation which she would otherwise have received in no stinted measure.

Accustomed to attach a wonderful amount of importance to duties and responsibilities which were his, if their due fulfilment could add to his dignity and reputation, Mr. Carruthers was a model of the uncle and guardian. He really liked Clare very much indeed, and he was fully persuaded that he loved her—a distinction he would have learned to draw only if Clare had been deprived of her possessions, and rendered dependent on him. He spoke of her as "my

brother's heiress," and so thought of her, not as
"my brother's orphan child;" but in all external
and material respects Mr. Carruthers of Poynings was an admirable guardian, and a highly
respectable specimen of the uncle tribe. He
would have been deeply shocked had he discovered that any young lady in the county was
better dressed, better mounted, more obsequiously
waited upon, more accomplished, or regarded by
society as in any way more favoured by fortune
than Miss Carruthers—not of Poynings, indeed,
but the next thing to it, and likely at some future
day to enjoy that distinction. Mr. Carruthers
did not regret that he was childless; he had
never cared for children, and, though not a
keenly observant person, he had noticed occasionally that the importance of a rich man's heir
was apt, in this irrepressibly anticipative world,
to outweigh the importance of the rich man himself. No Carruthers on record had ever had a
large family, and, for his own part, he liked the
idea of a female heir to the joint property of himself and his brother, who should carry her own
name in addition to her husband's. He was de-

termined on that. Unless Clare married a noble-
man, her husband should take the name of
Carruthers. Carruthers of Poynings must not
die out of the land. The strange jealousy which
was one of the underlying constituents of Mr.
Carruthers's character came into play with regard
to his niece and his wife. Mrs. Carruthers loved
the girl, and would gladly have acted the part of
a mother to her; and as Clare's own mother had
been a remarkably mild specimen of maternal
duty and affection, she could have replaced that
lady considerably to Clare's advantage. But she
had soon perceived that this was not to be; her
husband's fidgety sense of his own importance, his
ever-present fear lest it should be trenched upon
or in any way slighted, interfered with her good
intentions. She knew the uselessness of opposing
the foible, though she did not understand its
source, and she relinquished the projects she had
formed.

Mr. Carruthers was incapable of believing
that his wife never once dreamed of resenting
to Clare the exclusion of George, for which the
girl's residence at Poynings had been assigned as

a reason, or that she would have despised herself if such an idea had presented itself to her mind, as she probably must have despised him had she known how natural and inevitable he supposed it to be on her part.

Thus it came to pass that the three persons who lived together at Poynings had but little real intimacy or confidence between them. Clare was very happy; she had her own tastes and pursuits, and ample means of gratifying them. Her mother's brother and his wife, Sir Thomas and Lady Boldero, with her cousin, their ugly but clever and charming daughter, were much attached to her, and she to them, and, when she got away from Poynings to the Sycamores, Clare acknowledged to herself that she enjoyed the change very much, but was very happy at Poynings nevertheless. The Sycamores had another interest for her now, another association, and the girl's life had entered upon a new phase. Innocent, inexperienced, and romantic as she was, inclined to hero-worship, and by no means likely to form sound opinions as to her heroes, Clare Carruthers was endowed with an unusual allowance of common sense and perception. She understood Mr. Carruthers of Poynings thoroughly; so much more thoroughly than his wife, that she had found out the jealousy which permeated his character, and recognised it in action with unfailing accuracy. She had considerably more tact than girls at her age ordinarily possess, and she continued to fill a somewhat difficult position with satisfaction not only to others, but to herself. She contrived to avoid wounding her uncle's susceptible self-love, and to keep within the limits which Mrs. Carruthers's discretion had set to their intimacy, without throwing external coldness or restraint into their relations.

Clare found herself very often doing or not doing, saying or refraining from saying, some particular thing, in order to avoid "getting Mrs. Carruthers into a scrape," and of course she was aware that the constantly-recurring necessity for such carefulness argued, at the least, a difficult temper to deal with in the head of the household; but she did not let the matter trouble her much. She would think, when she thought about it at all, with the irrepressible self-complacency of youth,

how careful *she* would be not to marry an ill-
tempered man, or, at all events, she would make
up her mind to marry a man so devotedly attached to her that his temper would not be of
the slightest consequence, as, of course, she
should never suffer from it. On the whole, it
would be difficult to find a more dangerous condition of circumstances than that in which Clare
Carruthers was placed when her romantic meeting with Paul Ward took place—a meeting in
which the fates seemed to have combined every
element of present attraction and future danger.
Practically, Clare was quite alone; she placed
implicit confidence in no one, she had no guide
for her feelings or actions, and she had just
drifted into a position in which she needed careful direction. She had refrained from mentioning her meeting with the stranger, more on Mrs.
Carruthers's account than on her own, from the
usual motive—apprehension lest, by some unreasonable turn of Mr. Carruthers's temper, she
might be brought "into a scrape." Her curiosity had been strongly excited by the discovery
that Mrs. Carruthers had some sort of acquaint-

ance with Paul Ward, or, at least, with his name; but she adhered to her resolution, and kept silence for the present.

Mrs. Carruthers's son had always been an object of tacit interest to Clare. She had not been fully informed of the circumstances of her uncle's marriage, and she understood vaguely that George Dallas was an individual held in disfavour by the august master of Poynings; so her natural delicacy of feeling conquered her curiosity, and she abstained from mentioning George to his mother or to Mr. Carruthers, and also from giving encouragement to the gossip on the subject which occasionally arose in her presence.

In Mrs. Carruthers's dressing-room a portrait hung, which Clare had been told by Mrs. Brookes was that of her mistress's son, when a fine, brave, promising boy ten years old. Clare had felt an interest in the picture, not only for Mrs. Carruthers's sake, but because she liked the face which it portrayed—the clear bright brown eyes, the long curling hair, the brilliant dark complexion, the bold, frank, gleeful expression. Once or twice she had said a few words in praise of the picture, and once she had ventured to ask Mrs. Carruthers if her son still resembled it. The mother had answered her, with a sigh, that he was greatly changed, and no one would now recognise the picture as a likeness of him.

The dignified and decorous household at Poynings pursued its luxurious way with less apparent disunion among its principal members than is generally to be seen under the most favourable circumstances, but with little real community of feeling or of interest. Mrs. Carruthers was a popular person in society, and Clare was liked as much as she was admired. As for Mr. Carruthers, he was Mr. Carruthers of Poynings, and that fact sufficed for the neighbourhood almost as completely as it satisfied himself.

The unexpected return of her uncle from York had caused Clare no particular emotion. She was standing at the French window of the breakfast-room, feeding a colony of birds, her out-door pensioners, when the carriage made its appearance. She had just observed the fact, and was quietly pursuing her occupation, when Mrs.

Carruthers, who had left the breakfast-room half an hour before, returned, looking so pale, and with so unmistakable an expression of terror in her face, that Clare looked at her in astonishment.

"Your uncle has come back," she said. "I am not well, I cannot meet him yet. Go to the door, Clare, and tell him I am not well, and am still in my room. Pray go, my dear; don't delay a moment."

"Certainly I will go," answered Clare, leaving the window and crossing the room as she spoke; "but—"

"I'll tell you what ails me another time, but go now—go," said Mrs. Carruthers; and, without another word, the girl obeyed her. She had seen the carriage at a turn in the avenue; now the wheels were grinding the gravel of the sweep opposite the hall-door. In a minute Clare was receiving her uncle on the steps, and Mrs. Carruthers, having thrown the bonnet and shawl she had just taken out for her proposed expedition to the shrubbery back into the wardrobe, removed her gown, and replaced it by a dressing-gown, was awaiting her husband's approach with a beating heart and an aching head. Had he met her son? Had he passed him unseen upon the road? Would Mrs. Brookes succeed, unseen and unsuspected, in executing the commission with which she had hurriedly charged her?

"She is in a scrape of some sort," Clare thought, as she accompanied her uncle to his wife's dressing-room. "What can have happened since he left home? Can it have anything to do with Paul Ward?"

CHAPTER XII.

IT is nine o'clock in the morning, and breakfast is on the table in the pretty breakfast-room
at Poynings. Mrs. Carruthers presides over the
breakfast-table, and Clare is occupied in arranging
some flowers which have just been sent in by the
head gardener—sweet, fresh flowers, partaking
alike of the brightness of spring and the sweetness
of summer, for the April showers have fulfilled
their mission, and the earth is alike glowing and
redolent. Through the bow-window, opened in
fear and trembling by Clare before her uncle's
appearance, and hitherto unnoticed by that poten-
tate, who has a vivid dread of rheumatism, comes
a soft air laden with delicious scent of new-mown
grass; for close underneath three men are busily
engaged in trimming the broad lawn, and the
sound of their swiftly plied whetstones and the

hum of their talk in their occasional intervals of
rest has penetrated into the room, and makes a
kind of human accompaniment to Mr. Carruthers's
strictly unhuman and intonative manner of reading the morning prayers. Spreading far away, and
bordered in the extreme distance of a sloping
shoulder of Surrey down, lies the glorious Kentish
landscape, dotted here and there with broad red-
faced farmsteads and lowly labourers' cots, with
vast expanse of green and springing wheat and
hop-grounds, where the parasite has as yet scarcely
taken the tall poles within its pliant embrace, with
thick plantations and high chalk cuttings, over
which the steam from the flying train hangs like
a vaporous wreath. In the immediate neighbourhood of the house the big elm-trees, guarding on
either side the carriage-drive, tossed their high
heads and rustled their broad arms in all the delight
of their freshly acquired greenery; dew-bathed
broad upland and mossy knoll sparkle alike in the
morning sun; in the silvery bosom of the little lake
the reflection of the slowly-drifting clouds rears
quaint impalpable islands of strange fantastic form;
within the magic square of the old red kitchen-

garden wall, where rusty nails and fragments of last year's list still hung, large cucumber and melon frames blink in the sunlight, and every little hand-light lends a scintillating ray. Over all hangs a sense of stillness and composure, of peace and rest and quietude, such as might bring balm and healing to any wounded spirit.

External influences have, however, very little effect on one of the persons in the breakfast-room, for Mrs. Carruthers is bodily ill and mentally depressed. A racking nervous headache has deprived her of sleep during the past night, and has left its traces in deep livid marks underneath her eyes. She has a worn-out look and a preoccupied manner, and while she is superintending the preparation of the Grand Lama's tea—a process about which he is particular, and which is by no means to be lightly undertaken—her thoughts are far away, and her mind is full of doubts and misgiving. Why did her husband come back so suddenly from the agricultual meeting yesterday? Could he by any means have been aware of George's presence in the neighbourhood; and, if so, had he hastened his return with the view of detecting him? If so, he had providentially been thwarted in his plan. Nurse Ellen had seen the boy, and had conveyed to him the bracelet; the means of release from his surrounding difficulties were now in his hands, and the mother felt sure, from his manner, that he would keep his word, and never again subject himself to such a fearful risk. All danger surely must be over; no hint had been dropped by her husband of the slighest suspicion, and yet Mrs. Carruthers watches every change of his countenance, listens nervously to every footfall on the stairs, hears with a heart-beat the creak of every opening door, and is, obviously, constrained and wretched and ill at ease.

Clare notices this pityingly and with wonder; Mr. Carruthers notices it too, with wonder, but without any pity, but he resents it, in point of fact, silently and with dignity. That Mrs. Carruthers of Poynings should "mope" and be "out of sorts" is a kind of reflection on Mr. Carruthers of Poynings, which that gentleman by no means approves of. Over the top of his rustling newspaper he looks at his wife with severe glances levelled from under knitted brows; between his occasional bites of toast he gives a short, sharp, irritable cough;

now and then he drums with his fingers on the table, or taps his foot impatiently on the floor. No notice of these vagaries is taken by either of the ladies, it being generally understood at Poynings that the Grand Lama will always find vent in speech when the proper times arrives. Meanwhile, Mrs. Carruthers moodily broods over the breakfast equipage, and Clare continues her handiwork with the flowers.

The Grand Lama becomes more and more irate, glares through his gold double eye-glasses at the newspaper, wherein he is reading atrociously "levelling" views promulgated by a correspondent, gives utterance to smothered sounds indicative of indignation and contempt, and is just about to burst forth in a torrent of rage, when the door opens, and a footman, entering, hands a card on a salver to his master. As when, in full pursuit of the flying matador, the bull in the arena wheels round and engages the lithe picador who has just planted a flag-bearing dart in his quivering carcass, so Mr. Carruthers turns·upon the servant who had interposed between him and the intended objects of his attack.

"What's this?" said he, in a sharp voice.

"Card, sir," said the footman, utterly unmoved, and with the complacent expression of an ancient gurgoyle on a Saxon church.

"Do you think I'm blind?" said his master. "I see it's a card. Where did it come from?"

"Gentleman in the library, sir. Said you was at breakfast; told me no 'urry, and giv' me his card."

Mr. Carruthers looks up suspiciously at Thomas footman, but Thomas footman is still gurgoylesque. Then Mr. Carruthers replaces his eye-glasses, and, looking at the card, reads thereon, in old English characters, "Mr. Dalrymple," and in pencil the words "Home Office." "I will be with the gentleman in a moment." Only stopping at the looking-glass to run his fingers through his hair and to settle the tie of his checked cravat, Mr. Carruthers creaks out of the room.

Mr. Dalrymple, of the Home Office, has established himself in a comfortable chair, from which he rises on Mr. Carruthers's entrance. He is a tall, bald-headed man, and, to Mr. Carruthers's horror, wears a full-flowing brown beard. The

Grand Lama, whose ideas on this point are out of date, knows that beards are now generally worn by members of the aristocracy as well as foreigners and billiard-sharpers, but cannot conceive that any government has been so preposterously lax as to permit its officials to indulge in such nonsense. Consequently he refers to the card again, and, his first impressions being verified, is dumb with astonishment. Nevertheless, he controls his feelings sufficiently to bow and to point to a chair.

"I am an early visitor, Mr. Carruthers," says Mr. Dalrymple, "but the fact is, my business is pressing. I came down to Amherst by the mail-train last night, but I would not disturb you at so late an hour, and, moreover, I could have done no good by seeing you then; so I slept at the inn. My visit to you is on business, as I presume you understand?"

Mr. Dalrymple says this pointedly, as the Grand Lama's face is rapidly assuming an open mouth and sunken jaw expression of idiotcy. He recovers himself by an effort, and, glancing at the card, mutters "Home Office."

"Precisely," says Mr. Dalrymple. "I am a prin-

cipal clerk in the Home Office, and I come to you
in your capacity as justice of the peace. Lord
Wolstenholme, our Secretary, noticed that you
generally acted as chairman of the bench of magis-
trates, and therefore decided that you were the
proper person to be communicated with."

Mr. Carruthers's attention, which has been
wandering a little—his eyes are still attracted by
his visitor's beard, and he is wondering how long it
has been growing, and why it should be, as it is, of
two distinct shades of brown—is recalled by these
words, and he mutters that he is obliged to his
lordship for his opinion.

"Now, my dear Mr. Carruthers," says Mr.
Dalrymple, bending forward in his chair, dropping
his voice to a whisper, and looking slyly from
under his bushy eyebrows, "will you allow me to
ask you a question? Can you keep a secret?"

Mr. Carruthers is taken aback. From his
magisterial and county-gentleman position he
looks upon secrets as things exclusively appertain-
ing to the vulgar, as connected with conspiracies,
plots, swindles, and other indictable offences. Considering, however, that the matter is brought

under his notice in connection with the Home Office, he thinks he may venture to answer in the affirmative, and does accordingly.

"Ex-actly," says Mr. Dalrymple. "I knew your answer before I put the question; but in these little matters it is absolutely necessary to have perfect accuracy. Now then to the point— we are quite out of earshot? Thank you! No chance of any one listening at the doors?"

Mr. Carruthers says "No," with an expression of face which says he should very much like to catch any one there.

"Pre-cisely! Now, my dear Mr. Carruthers, I will at once put you in possession of Lord Wolstenholme's views. The fact is, that a murder has been committed, under rather peculiar circumstances, and his lordship wants your assistance in investigating the matter."

Mr. Carruthers is all attention in an instant. Every trace of pre-occupation has vanished. His visitor's beard has no kind of attraction for him now, though it is wagging close before his eyes. A murder! The worst case he had ever investigated was a doubtful manslaughter arising out of a poaching affray, and for his remarks on that he had been highly complimented in the local press; but here is murder—and his aid is enlisted by the Home Office!

"The facts of the case," continues Mr. Dalrymple, "are shortly these. A body of a man is seen floating off Paul's Wharf, and is hooked up by one of the men attached to the steam-boat pier there. It is taken to the police-station to be examined, and is then found to have been stabbed to the heart with a sharp instrument, and by a strong and clever hand. The pockets are empty, the studs have been taken from the shirt, and there is no token, pocket-book, or anything to establish its identity. 'Ordinary case enough,' you'll say, with your experience; 'ordinary case enough—drunken man decoyed into some water-side ken, robbed, and made away with—case for the police—why Lord Wolstenholme and the Home Office?' You would say that, my dear sir, influenced by your ordinary perspicacity; but I answer your 'Why.' From the appearance of this man's body, it is plain that he was not an Englishman; his clothes are not of English cut, and he had on a huge fur-lined overcoat, with a deep hood, such as no Englishman ever wears. When this description was sent to us, Lord Wolstenholme at once referred to a private correspondence which we have had with the French embassy in relation to some of the Second-of-December exiles who are now sheltered under the British flag, and we came to the conclusion that this was no common murder for purposes of plunder, but an act of political vengeance. Now, my dear sir, you will perceive that to penetrate a mystery of this kind is of the greatest political importance, and consequently his lordship took the matter up at once, and set every engine we have at work to elucidate it. The result of our inquiries proves that the whole chance of identification rests upon a question of coats. The last person by whom, so far as we know, the wearer of the fur-lined coat was seen alive is a waiter at a tavern in the Strand, who distinctly recollects the murdered man, whose dress he described very fully, being particularly positive about his jewelry—diamond studs, real, no 'duffers,' as he said, and of which there is no trace to be found—having dined at his eating-house, in company with another man, who had with him a blue Witney overcoat, on the inside of which was a label bearing the name of some tailor, Ewart or Evans, he is unable to state which, residing at Amherst."

" Good God !" said Mr. Carruthers, surprised out of his usual reticence. " Evans—I know the man well !"

" Very likely !" says Mr. Dalrymple, composedly. " Evans ! The waiter has been had up, cross-questioned, turned inside out, but still adheres to his story. Now, as we imagine this to be a bit of political vengeance, and not an ordinary crime, and as the detectives (capital fellows in their way) have had their heads a little turned since they've been made novel heroes of, Lord Wolstenholme thought it better that I should come down into the neighbourhood of Amherst, and with your assistance try to find out where and by whom this coat was bought."

No hesitation now on Mr. Carruthers's part; he and the Home Office are colleagues in this affair. Lord Wolstenholme has shown his sagacity in picking out the active and intelligent magistrate of the district, and he shall see that his confidence is not misplaced. Will Mr. Dalrymple breakfast? Mr. Dalrymple has breakfasted; then a message is sent to Mrs. Carruthers to say that Mr. Carruthers presumes he *may* say that Mr. Dalrymple, a gentleman from London, will join them at dinner? Mr. Dalrymple will be delighted, so long as he catches the up-mail train at Amherst at—what is it?—nine fifteen. Mr. Carruthers pledges his word that Mr. Dalrymple shall be in time, and orders the barouche round at once. Will Mr. Dalrymple excuse Mr. Carruthers for five minutes? Mr. Dalrymple will; and Mr. Carruthers goes to his dressing-room, while Mr. Dalrymple re-ensconces himself in the big arm-chair, and devotes his period of solitude to paring his nails and whistling softly the while.

The big, heavy, swinging barouche, only used on solemn occasions, such as state visits, Sunday church-goings, and magisterial sittings, drawn by the two big grays, and driven by Gibson, coachman, in his silver wig, his stiff collar, and his bright top-boots, and escorted by Thomas, footman, in all the bloom of blue-and-silver livery and drab gaiters, comes round to the front door, and the gentlemen take their places in it and are driven off. The three gardeners mowing the lawn perform Hindooish obeisances as the carriage passes them; obeisances acknowledged by Mr. Carruthers with a fore-finger lifted to the brim of his hat, as modelled on a portrait of the late Duke of Wellington. Bulger at the lodge gates pulls his forelock, and receives the same gracious return, Mr. Carruthers all the time bristling with the sense of his own importance, and inwardly wishing that he could tell gardeners, lodge-keeper, and every one they met that his companion had come from the Home Office, and that they were about together to investigate a most important case of murder. Mr. Dalrymple, on the contrary, seems to have forgotten all about the actual business under treatment, and might be a friend come on a few days' visit. He admires the scenery, asks about the shooting, gives his opinion on the rising crops, talks of the politics rife in the neighbourhood, showing, by the way, a keen knowledge of their details, and never for an instant refers to the object of their inquiry until they are nearing the town, when he suggests that they had better

alight short of their destination, and proceed on
foot there. There is no particular reason for this,
as probably Mr. Dalrymple knows; but he has
never yet pursued an official and mysterious investigation in a barouche, and it seems to him an
abnormal proceeding. So Mr. Carruthers defer-
ring in a courtly manner to his visitor's wishes, but,
at the same time, walking beside him as though
he had him in charge, they alight from the carriage, bidding the servant to wait, and walk into the
town, directing their steps towards Evans, tailor.

Evans, tailor, coatless, as is his wont, and with
his thumbs stuck in the arm-holes of his waistcoat, is standing at his door, and greets Mr. Carruthers with as much bow as is possible to his
stout figure. Could they speak to him for a moment? by all manner of means; will Mr. Carruthers walk into the back shop? where Miss Evans,
a buxom girl with many shaking curls, is discovered working a pair of Berlin-wool slippers, at a
glance too small for her father, and is put to flight
with much blushing and giggling. The two gentlemen seat themselves in the old-fashioned black-
horsehair chairs, and Mr. Evans, a little excited,

stands by them with his thumbs in his arm-holes, and flaps his hands occasionally, as though they were fins.

"This gentleman, Mr. Evans," says Mr. Carruthers, giving this happy specimen of his acumen and discretion in a loud and pompous tone—"has come from Lord Wolstenholme, the Secretary of State for the Home Department." Mr. Evans gives a fin-flap, indicative of profound respect. "He has been sent here to—"

"Will you permit me in the very mildest manner to interrupt you, my dear sir?" says Mr. Dalrymple, in dulcet accents. "You put the matter admirably from the magisterial point of view—but perhaps if I were just to— You have no objection? Thank you! You've lived a long time in Amherst, Mr. Evans?"

"I've been a master tailor here, sir, forty-three years last Michaelmas."

"Forty-three years! Long time, indeed! And you're the tailor of the neighbourhood, eh?"

"Well, sir, I think I may say we make for all the gentry round—Mr. Carruthers of Poynings, sir, and Sir Thomas Boldero, and—"

" Of course—of course ! You've a gold-printed label, I think, which you generally sew on to all goods made by you ?"

" We have, sir—that same. With my name upon it."

" With your name upon it. Just so ! Now, I suppose that label is never sewed on to anything which has not been either made or sold by you?"

" Which has not been made, sir ! We don't sell anything except our own make—Evans of Amherst don't."

" Exactly ; and very proper too." To Mr. Carruthers : " Settles one point, my dear sir—must have been made here ! Now, Mr. Evans, you make all sorts of coats, of course, blue Witney overcoats among the number ?"

Mr. Evans, after a hesitating fin-flap, says : " A blue Witney overcoat, sir, is a article seldom if ever called for in these parts. I shouldn't say we'd made one within the last two years—leastways, more than one."

" But you think you did make one ?"

" There were one, sir, made to order from a party that was staying at the Lion."

"Staying at the Lion? The inn, of course, where I slept last night. How long ago was that?"

"That were two years ago, sir."

"That won't do!" cries Mr. Dalrymple, in disappointed tone.

"Two years ago that it were made and that the party was at the Lion. The coat was sold less than three months ago."

"Was it? To whom?"

"To a stranger—a slim young gent who came in here one day promiscuous, and wanted an overcoat. He had that blue Witney, he had!"

"Now, my dear Mr. Evans," says Mr. Dalrymple, laying his hand lightly on Mr. Evans's shirt-sleeve, and looking up from under his bushy brows into the old man's face," just try and exercise your memory a little about this stranger. Give us a little more description of him—his age, height, general appearance, and that sort of thing!"

But Mr. Evans's memory is quite unaccustomed to exercise, and cannot be jogged, or ensnared, or bullied into any kind of action. The

stranger was young, "middling height," appearance, "well, gen-teel and slim-like;" and wild
horses could not extract further particulars from
Mr. Evans than these. Stay. "What did he
give for the coat, and in what money did he pay
for it?" There's a chance. Mr. Evans remem-
bers that he "gev fifty-three-and-six for the overcoat, and handed in a ten-pun' note for change.
A ten-pound note, which, as Mr. Evans, by a further tremendous effort, recollects, had "the stamp
of our post-office on it, as I pinted out to the gent
at the time." Was the note there? No; Mr.
Evans had paid it into the County Bank to his
little account with some other money, but he quite
recollected the post-office stamp being on it.

Mr. Carruthers thinks this a great point, but
is dashed by Mr. Dalrymple's telling him, on
their way from the tailor's, that all bank-notes
passing through post-offices receive the official
stamp. This statement is corroborated at the Amherst post-office, where no money-order of that
amount, or of anything equivalent to that amount,
has been recently paid, the remittances in that
form being, as the postmaster explains, generally

to the canal boatmen or the railway people, and of small value.

So there the clue fails suddenly and entirely, and Mr. Carruthers and Mr. Dalrymple again mount the big swinging barouche and are driven back to Poynings to dinner, which meal is not, however, graced by the presence of either of the ladies; for Mrs. Carruthers is too ill to leave her room, and Clare is in attendance on her. So the gentlemen eat a solemn dinner by themselves, and talk a solemn conversation; and at eight o'clock Mr. Dalrymple goes away, driven by Gibson, coachman, in the carriage, and turning over in his mind how best to make something out of the uneventful day for the information of the Home Secretary.

That dignitary occupies also much of the attention of Mr. Carruthers, left in dignified solitude in the dining-room before the decanters of wine and the dishes of fruit, oblivious of his wife's indisposition, and wholly unobservant of the curiosity with which Mr. Downing, his butler and body-servant, surveys him on entering the room to suggest the taking of tea. Very unusual is it

for the Poynings servants to regard their master
with curiosity, or indeed with any feeling that
bears the semblance of interest; but, be the cause
what it may, there is no mistaking the present
expression of Downing's face. Surprise, curiosity,
and something which, if it must be called fear, is
the pleasant and excited form of that feeling,
prompt Mr. Downing to look fixedly at his master, who sits back in his chair in an attitude of
magisterial cogitation, twirling his heavy gold eye-
glass in his bony white hands, and lost in something which resembles thought more closely than
Mr. Carruthers's mental occupation can ordinarily
be said to do. There he sits, until he resolves to
take his niece Clare into confidence, tell her of
the visit he has received from the gentleman from
the Home Office, and ask her whether she can
make anything of it, which resolution attained,
and finding by his watch that the hour is half-
past ten, and that therefore a Carruthers of Poynings may retire to rest if he chooses without in-
decorum, the worthy gentleman creaks up-stairs
to his room, and in a few minutes is sleeping the
sleep of the just. Mrs. Carruthers—Clare having

been some time previously dismissed from the room—also seems to sleep soundly; at least her husband has seen that her eyes are closed.

Her rest, real or pretended, would have been none the calmer had she been able to see her faithful old servant pacing up and down the housekeeper's room, and wringing her withered hands in an agony of distress; for the servant who had gone to Amherst with Mr. Carruthers and his mysterious visitor in the morning had learned the meaning and purpose of the two gentlemen's visit to Evans, the tailor, and had made it the subject of a lively and sensational conversation in the servants' hall. Although literature was not in a very flourishing condition at Amherst, the male domestics of the household at Poynings were not without their sources of information, and had thoroughly possessed themselves of the details of the murder.

Mrs. Brookes had heard of the occurrence two or three times in the course of the preceding day but she had given it little attention. She was in her own room when the servants returned with the carriage which had taken Mr. Dalrymple to the railway station, having visited her mistress for the last time that evening, and was thinking, sadly enough, of George, when the entrance of the upper housemaid, her eager.face brimful of news, disturbed her.

"O, Mrs. Brookes," she began, "do you know who that gentleman was as dined here, and went to the town with master?"

"No, I don't," said Mrs. Brookes, with some curiosity; "do you?"

"Not exactly; but Thomas says Home Office were wrote on his card, and Home Office has something to do with finding people out when they've been a-doing anything."

Mrs. Brookes began to feel uncomfortable.

"What do you mean?" she said. "Who's been doing anything that wants finding out?"

"Nobody as I knows," replied Martha, looking knowing and mysterious. "Only, you know, that murder as Mr. Downing read us the inquest of, and how it's a foreigner as has been killed because he wouldn't help to blow up the King of France; at least, there's something of that in it.

Well, Mr. Downing thinks as the gentleman come about that."

"About that, *here?*" said Mrs. Brookes. "Whatever has put such a notion into Mr. Downing's head as that?"

"Well, Mrs. Brookes, this is it: they're all talking about it in the hall, and so I thought I'd just come and tell you. Master and the stranger gentleman didn't take the carriage right on into town; they got just inside the pike, and went on by themselves; and, when they came back, master he looked very red and grand-looking, and the strange gentleman he looked as if he was rare disappointed and put out, and, as he was a-shutting the door of the b'rouche, Thomas heard him saying, 'No, no; there's nothing more to be done. Evans was our only chance, and he's no use.' So nat'rally Thomas wonders whatever they've been about, and what was their business with Evans; so he and coachman wasn't sorry this evening when the strange gentleman was gone by the train, and they see Evans a-loung-in' about, a-flapping his hands, which he's always

doing of it, up by the station. He were lookin'
at the strange gentleman as sharp as sharp, as
they drove up to the bookin'-office; and when
they came out, there he were, and Evans tells 'em
all about it."

" All about *what?*" asks Mrs. Brookes, sharply.

" All about what brought master and the other
gentleman to his shop; and it's his belief, as master said more than the other gentleman wanted
him to say; for master let out as how a murder
had something to do with the business."

" What business, Martha? Do tell me what
you mean, if you want me to listen to you any
longer. How could Mr. Carruthers want to know
anything from Evans about a murder?"

" Lor', ma'm, it weren't about the murder;
it were about the coat! Master told Evans as
how there had been a murder, and the other
gentleman took master up rather shorter, Evans
thinks, than master is accustomed to be took,
and asked him no end of questions—did he make
such and such coats? and who did he sell 'em to?
and partic'lar did he sell Witney coats? which

Mr. Evans said he didn't in general, and had only sold one in two years, which the strange gentleman wanted to know what sort of gent had had it, and were he young or old, or good-looking or or'nary, and a mort of questions; wherein Evans answered him to the best of his ability, but, being a man of his word, he couldn't make it no clearer than he could."

"What *did* he make clear?" asked Mrs. Brookes. "Two years is a long time to remember the sale of a coat."

"It wasn't so long since it were sold. Mr. Evans sold it six weeks ago, but it were two years made."

Mrs. Brookes's heart gave a great bound, and her old eyes grew dim; but she was a brave woman, and Martha, housemaid, was a dull one.

"Did Mr. Evans not succeed in describing the person who bought the coat, then?"

"He thinks not; but he says he should know him again immediate, if he saw him. The strange gentleman didn't seem over-pleased that his memory was so short; but lor', who's to know all about the eyeses and the noses of everybody as comes to buy a coat, or what not?—partic'lar if you don't know as he's been a committen of a murder. If you did, why, you'd look at him closer like, *I* should say!"

"Has Mr. Downing got the paper with the murder of the foreigner in it?" asked Mrs. Brookes.

"Yes, he have; he's just been reading it all over again in the hall. And he says as how master's in a brown study, as he calls it; only it's in the dining-room, and he's sure as the finding-out people has put it into his hands."

"When he has done with the paper, ask him to let me see it, Martha. Very likely this stranger's visit has nothing to do with the matter. Downing finds out things that nobody else can see."

Martha was an admirer and partisan of Mr. Downing, from the humble and discreet distance which divides a housemaid from a butler, and she did not like to hear his discretion aspersed.

"It looks as if he was right this time, however," she replied; "though it wasn't Tim the

tinker as stole Sir Thomas's spoons, which Mr.
Downing never had a good opinion of him; but
when there ain't nothing clearer than the person
who was seen at the eating-house with the vic-
tim" (Martha "took in" the *Hatchet of Horror*
every week, and framed her language on that
delightful model) "had on a coat as Evans made,
it looks as if he wasn't altogether in the wrong,
now don't it, Mrs. Brookes?"

Mrs. Brookes could not deny that it looked
very like that complimentary conclusion, and her
brave old heart almost died within her. But she
kept down her fear and horror, and dismissed
Martha, telling her to bring her the paper as
soon as she could. The woman returned in a
few moments, laid the newspaper beside Mrs.
Brookes, and then went off to enjoy a continua-
tion of the gossip of the servants' hall. Very
exciting and delightful that gossip was, for
though the servants had no inkling of the terri-
bly strong interest, the awfully near connection,
which existed for Poynings in the matter, it was
still a great privilege to be "in" so important an

affair by even the slender link formed by the probable purchase of a coat at Amherst by the murderer. They enjoyed it mightily; they discussed it over and over again, assigning to the murdered man every grade of rank short of royalty, and all the virtues possible to human nature. The women were particularly eloquent and sympathising, and Martha "quite cried," as she speculated on the great probability of there being a broken-hearted sweetheart in the case.

In the housekeeper's room, Mrs. Brookes sat poring over the terrible story, to which she had listened carelessly on the previous day, as the servants talked it vaguely over. From the first words Martha had spoken, her fears had arisen, and now they were growing every instant to the terrible certainty of conviction. What if the wretched young man, who had already been the cause of so much misery, had added this fearful crime to the long catalogue of his follies and sins?

All the household sleeps, and the silence of the night is in every room but one. There Mrs.

Brookes still sits by the table with the newspaper spread before her, lost in a labyrinth of fear and anguish; and from time to time her grief finds words, such as:

"How shall I tell her? How shall I warn her? O George, George! O my boy! my boy!"

END OF VOL. I.

LONDON:
ROBSON AND SON, GREAT NORTHERN PRINTING WORKS,
PANCRAS ROAD, N.W.